CAUGHT UP
IN LOVE

C. A. KRAUSE

FOREWORD

To my readers,

This book is a work of fiction and the events in it take place much quicker than they tend to in real life. Remember, trust needs time and should never be rushed. I do not recommend readers attempt any of the practices found in this book based on my descriptions. Again, this is a work of fiction and is only intended for my readers' entertainment, not for educational purposes.

That being said, I very much hope you enjoy the story and characters.

I appreciate every one of you!

C.A.

CHAPTER ONE

Tax season was probably the worst time of year for every small business owner, but Jessica doubted it was as awkward for anyone else as it was for her. Being a BDSM club owner in a rural neighborhood definitely posed some challenges.

Since she'd stubbornly decided to overcome the rural prejudice that she'd faced when first opening Club B amidst the farms and small town businesses thirty minutes outside of Toronto, she only shopped in the local stores and used services offered by other business people in the area. It had worked out for the most part. People respected that she supported them by not taking her business to the large corporate stores that sold similar products much cheaper.

And, since she had absolutely no intention of dealing with the convoluted tax forms the government required, one of the first services she'd needed to secure two years ago when she'd moved here, had been a tax adviser. It had probably been too much to hope for that there would be a young liberally minded person running the local accounting firm.

Drawing herself up and plastering a smile on her face, she rang the doorbell of the two-story house that held the offices of the no-nonsense man in his fifties that had grudgingly accepted her business.

"Good afternoon. I have an appointment to sign my income tax papers."

"Good morning, Ms. Levington." The receptionist greeted her with a scrutinizing look on her face. It was the same look Jessica had gotten used to. She supposed people tried to figure out why a relatively young, respectable looking woman had brought a club of questionable morality to their church fearing midst. It didn't bother her anymore, just like the shocked and sometimes derisive looks she'd gotten when she'd first moved here simply bounced off of her. On most days, anyway.

Over the past two years, people had gotten used to her being around town, and while gossip occasionally still followed her, the novelty of her club had worn off and her neighbors had apparently realized that she wasn't about to walk around in a corset, swinging a whip and flogger. Unfortunately, the receptionist here was an exception to that rule and had Jessica working hard to maintain her neutral expression.

"You can take a seat in the conference room. Mr. Garris will be there in a moment. Would you like tea, coffee, or water?"

"A water would be great, thank you." There was still hope that she wouldn't be here long enough for a hot drink. Sign and bail. That sounded good to her.

Just as she sank into one of the rather uncomfortable chairs standing around the oval meeting desk, Mr. Garris walked in.

"Ms. Levington, hello."

Jessica rose to shake the man's hand. After he held her chair out for her, he lowered himself into the one next to hers. With a loud thud, he placed some papers on the table in front of them. The call of misery, if Jessica had ever heard it. At least, Mr. Garris wasted no time chit chatting. Jessica assumed he just wasn't the type, though perhaps he just didn't know what to say to his most infamous client. The thought should have been amusing, if their meetings didn't always end up being terribly awkward.

Explaining to her tax advisor why she'd purchased ginger roots in December had probably been even more uncomfortable than listing the new fucking machine she'd bought in the fall. He'd suggested that if she had events that involved purchasing refreshments herself, she should have kept the receipts for the other foods and drinks he assumed she'd paid for, adding them to the monthly catering bill she always included in her tax filings. Jessica was certain that the man had been close to a heart attack when she'd explained that the ginger roots hadn't been purchased as a refreshment item.

Poor Mr. Garris had gone so red she'd immediately regretted not simply nodding and apologizing for her oversight in saving the other receipts. Her friend Vivienne had later joked that Mr. Garris had probably gone online and searched for ginger root uses after speaking with Jessica and had inadvertently learned all about figging. That thought had been enough for Jessica to consider taking her business to someone in the city, after all.

But she'd decided against it, and today she'd hopefully be spared any further embarrassments. Then she could leave this office and not return for another year, relying solely on emails to send all her accounting to Mr. Garris' office each month.

"You've made a significant profit last year, so you are looking at paying a bit of income tax." He pointed out the respective lines on the tax forms and spend the next fifteen minutes going over some details, before Jessica could finally place her signature on the paper and say her goodbyes. It had been a surprisingly painless meeting, after all.

"Thank you for coming in today, Ms. Levington," Mr. Garris said as he walked her to the front door.

"Yes, thank you, Mr. Garris. I'll just continue to email you my receipts and you'll contact me if there are any questions?"

Averting his eyes, the older man coughed and nodded at the same time. Jessica took this as her cue to depart quickly. No need to witness Mr. Garris remembering the plethora of sex toys, lube, and fetish gear receipts he had received over the past two years.

Waving at the judgmental receptionist, she stepped outside and took a deep breath. She loved her club, and she wasn't ashamed of being associated with the BDSM lifestyle, but that didn't mean that being a bondage club owner in a relatively conservative rural area didn't add pressure to the already challenging task of managing a business all by herself.

Luckily, plenty of her members didn't mind the drive from the city and preferred the exclusivity of her club. And tonight, she'd finally have time to let go of some of that pressure, because tonight was Club B's Valentine's Day party that she'd looked forward to for weeks. With all the preparations that'd gone into it, it was bound to be a success, even if she'd be busy overseeing the kinky game they'd planned for tonight instead of finding herself a dom to play with.

A few hours later, Jessica watched as a half-naked woman hurled herself over a spanking bench, frantically trying to duck behind it to avoid the toy arrow a dom had shot in her direction. The woman failed and the arrow hit her shoulder, leaving turquoise paint on the sub's skin as it fell to the ground. The shout of victory that the dom standing on the sidelines let out made Jessica simultaneously want to grin and give the sub a sympathetic hug. Looked like the woman had more spanking benches in her future.

The kinky obstacle course, where submissives had to evade the toy arrows shot by the doms, had been a great idea. Jessica had wanted to do something special and fun for her club's party and, clearly, she'd succeeded. Everyone seemed to love the party game, and upstairs, those who had played in the first round were probably busy reaping their rewards.

Only Jessica and a couple of helpers were down here, not actively playing. Of course, her helpers were taking turns tonight, so that each of them could play in one round of the game at least. Only Jessica wouldn't, as was so often the case. The downside of owning a BDSM club, as opposed to just being a member.

"Excuse me, Jessica?" Jordie's voice interrupted her focus on the naked people in front of her. Over the yells and laughter coming from the obstacle course, she hadn't heard her bartender approach and she let out a startled yelp, momentarily looking away from the race.

"Hold on, I have to pay attention and see who crosses the finish line first."

The game had two objectives for the bottoms and submissives. They had to be the first one to cross the course, and they also needed to avoid getting shot by a dom while they were racing over, under, and around the obstacles.

Those submissives in a committed relationship, even if it was just for the night, might have also been given a time to beat, their doms holding stopwatches. Whatever additional challenges the doms had given their submissives, there were currently fifteen people in various states of undress racing toward her, and Jessica kept her eyes on the finish line to see which one of them would cross it first.

The bouncing breasts and male parts were quite an amusing display, and the doms who were holding their bows and arrows like hunters preparing to take down their prey all looked like they were kids in a candy store. There would most definitely be a lot of licking and ravishing going on tonight.

Crawling under a line of three saw horses, two women were fighting for the lead, one of them hindered by her rather big bust. When the second, less-busty one pushed herself up on the other side and raced over the finish line, Jessica blew her whistle and declared her the winner.

Turning to Jordie, she gave him a questioning look. "Is there something wrong at the bar?"

"Not at all, but Mistress Vivienne sent me down here to take over your place for the last round of the game."

Jessica stared at Jordie, who just looked back, obviously much less confused than her. "Did she say what she needed me for?"

Her best friend was a well-respected domme in the club and also the event planner Jessica had hired to set up everything she'd needed for tonight's party. Hopefully, there had been no unforeseen problems come up that she needed to deal with. She'd really hoped tonight would go by smoothly, perhaps even allowing her to relax a bit after the game and actually mingle with her friends or look for a play partner.

If she ever wanted to find a dom for herself, she needed to be more proactive in looking for someone who might be a suitable match. A task that seemed daunting, considering she already knew almost everyone in the club personally, and even though she thought her club members liked her well-enough, she also knew she'd gained a reputation among the doms. It was hard to be suitably submissive when you also owned the place and could correct many of the newer doms on their techniques and use of the equipment.

"No, sorry, she just told me to relieve you." Jordie interrupted her thoughts.

"And that is where I come in," a second voice said from behind her bartender.

Master Benjamin stepped up to them, giving Jessica an assessing look. "It appears your friend felt you ought to be allowed a chance to experience the obstacle course for yourself."

Jessica felt herself blink at him and heat shot to her face. Ever since the man had shown up at her club last weekend, she couldn't stop blushing each time he said something to her. For a woman who owned a bondage club, this blushing thing was getting damned embarrassing. In fact, it was embarrassing enough that she was now second guessing her wisdom in allowing him to by-pass the wait list.

She'd granted Master Benjamin, a well-known and respected dom, an immediate membership in exchange for his taking over the role of dungeon monitor during tonight's party, and at the time it had seemed like the perfect solution to her staffing problem for the evening. That had been before she'd met him in person.

A disconcerting thought crossed her mind. "And why are you here?"

The only change in his expression was a tiny twitch of the corner of his mouth. He held up a toy bow. "To hunt, of course."

"But you are the dungeon monitor upstairs?" It came out as a question, and Jessica wanted to give herself a shake. She knew perfectly well that Master Benjamin should be upstairs helping monitor the scenes going on, since she was the one who'd assigned him to do just that. It was the reason she'd let him start his membership here right away. She'd needed a monitor badly, and he'd come with the highest recommendation from a respected dom she knew personally.

Except now he was down here, not wearing the white trimmed vest she'd handed him earlier.

"Mistress Vivienne has kindly taken over that duty. She's also asked me to remind you that she is perfectly capable of monitoring the floor for an hour," he explained, easing her brewing irritation slightly. She'd told him to follow all of Vivienne's instructions tonight. Since Vivienne had planned the party, knew Jessica's expectations, and Jessica herself was occupied down here, it had made sense to tell Benjamin that Vivienne would let him know if there was something he should do.

But what was Vivienne thinking?

"An hour?" Jessica was certain her expression conveyed the sinking feeling of realization she was experiencing. She looked over to the club members who were now pairing up, ready to head upstairs and celebrate the victors. Everyone looked excited and some submissives a bit worried. It was the perfect mix of anxiety and lust that made being in a dungeon so intoxicating.

How long had it been since she'd had the chance to let loose? Tonight's atmosphere was the perfect opportunity to finally get lost in a scene again. Just moments before, she'd thought about how she needed to put herself out there more. Sure, Master Benjamin wouldn't have been her first choice of play partner, but it was only for one hour and she knew he had a solid reputation and track record in the community. It was the reason she'd given him a membership in the first place. His background had checked out perfectly, and no one would ever say she wasn't thorough in checking up on every one of her club's members.

It had all been a rather fortunate coincidence. Master Hell, who owned a BDSM club in L.A., had called her, letting her know that Master Benjamin was moving to Canada, hoping to join her club. Since she'd known Master Hell would never give a reference for someone not worthy of her trust, she'd agreed to add Master Benjamin to her wait list without insisting on a personal interview first.

After they'd chatted for a bit about their clubs, Jessica had mentioned her desperate search for a new dungeon monitor, especially for the upcoming party where she would need help badly, and Master Hell had made a suggestion. Instead of adding Master Benjamin to the wait list, which admittedly would have meant a rather lengthy wait before he'd actually get to join the club, Master Benjamin would step in as a dungeon monitor in exchange for being allowed to join the club right away.

It had seemed like the perfect solution. Apparently, he'd done dungeon monitor duties on occasion at Master Hell's dungeon as a favor to the owner, so he knew what he'd need to look out for during a shift. Given that she'd been in dire need of a well-qualified and experienced dungeon monitor and the two other references Master Benjamin had supplied upon request had checked out, she'd agreed.

So now Master Benjamin was in her club, staring at her like he had all the time in the world for her to give him an answer. Except, when she tried to figure out how to answer him, she realized he hadn't actually asked her anything. And wasn't that the problem? The man oozed dominance and every time she had to talk with him, she felt as if she should respond to some unspoken expectation and each time she fell short because she couldn't figure out what to do. It was unnerving, especially since technically she was his boss, at least for tonight.

"Are you suggesting that she sent you down here to shoot at me?"

Now his mouth twitched a bit more, almost as if he was trying very hard not to make fun of her. "Indeed, she did. I must say, your friend can be quite convincing. I can see why she has such an excellent reputation as a domme."

What in the world had Vivienne said to Master Benjamin? She'd have to grill her friend about this later, but right now she needed to make a choice. Join the game she'd set up for her members and have some fun herself, or send Master Benjamin and Jordie on their way and explain why she'd done it to Vivienne later. And wouldn't that be a great conversation? Experienced submissive and club owner running to her best friend to whine about wanting a dom for herself when she couldn't even bring herself to give the men who were willing to scene with her a decent shot because they made her nervous.

She knew what she wanted to do. She wanted to get a chance to play, even if the idea of a scene with Master Benjamin was disconcerting, to say the least. It would be one step in the right direction to overcome her reluctance to actually submit to the eligible doms in the club. If she truly wanted to have another relationship in the future, she needed to take some chances.

"Okay." The word was out before she could think better of it.

An appreciative look entered Master Benjamin's eyes, and somehow that equally thrilled and worried her. She reminded herself that they had a one-hour time limit. She could let go of her worries for an hour and enjoy herself. Afterward, she could leave and decide whether this had been a great or a terrible idea.

CHAPTER TWO

Jessica handed Jordie the whistle and gave him instructions for the game, then she checked the time. It was eleven forty-five. Assuming it had been about ten minutes since Vivienne had taken over the dungeon monitor duties, they had until twelve thirty together.

"Let's go, Jessica." Master Benjamin took her hand, and for the first time, he actually smiled at her. "We need to get you naked before the game starts, so I can properly enjoy watching you."

He pulled her to the side of the room, where he stepped behind her, placing his hands on her shoulders. She didn't mind nudity, but the weight of his hands on her sent tingles down her back. Lifting her hands, she started to untie her white baby doll lingerie. With a huff, Master Benjamin pushed her hands aside.

"Just stand still. I'm not in the habit of letting my subs take over all the fun parts. Undressing the beautiful women I play with is a treat I rarely miss out on."

The compliment calmed her nerves slightly, and she lowered her hands, allowing Master Benjamin to loosen the small ribbons that held her skimpy outfit together. He had large hands, but no calluses. His paperwork said he was self-employed in something finance related. Still, his build was large and muscular and he towered over her. Not that it was particularly hard, given her less than average five foot six height. She had to wonder whether he preferred bigger women who had large breasts like the submissive on the obstacle course earlier. Breasts his hands could grab and hold, rather than her small ones.

"Hmmm, I do like your shape, little one. You're so very small, I could easily hold you down with very little effort and do so many interesting things to you." He said it sounding absent-minded, while he pulled the straps of her lingerie down over her shoulders, relieving her of her unspoken concerns.

She'd agreed to do this game with him and have some fun today, so she forced her mind to focus on his movements instead of getting caught up in insecurities. She was old enough to know better than to compare herself to other women. She was here with him, and Master Benjamin didn't strike her as the type of dom who did anything that he didn't truly want to, which meant he was here because he wanted to play with her. The thought made her skin grow heated.

As he pulled her lingerie down, his fingers left her feeling tingly and nerves flared to life with his touch, as if he'd flipped a simple switch in her body. His hands slid down her back to her tight latex boy shorts. Without stopping, he pulled them down, nudging her leg to step out of them. Now she was completely naked, and Master Benjamin's hands ran up and down the backs of her thighs.

Jessica felt her thoughts quiet down completely. Master Benjamin didn't waste time talking, he simply took control of her body. Her entire attention pivoted to the trail of heat his fingertips left on her skin. She allowed herself to close her eyes, permitting him to take charge of her.

His fingers stopped moving, and he removed his hands from her completely. Her eyes sprung open and, after blinking, she realized everyone was organizing themselves for the third and last round of the obstacle course.

"Let's get you to the start line. You don't need to worry about anything other than crossing that finish line before I shoot you with this little toy arrow here. If you cross it without being shot, then you won. If I shoot you, which I know I will, I'll reward myself quite nicely." With that, he pushed her naked ass in the direction of the starting line.

"But if I cross the line before you shoot me, I'll get to choose a reward," she said, feeling compelled to remind him of the rule of the game. Submissives who weren't shot could ask their doms for a reward instead.

Master Benjamin just laughed. "Don't get your hopes up, little one."

She watched him walk unhurriedly to the side of the room, where all the dom/mes lined up with their bows and arrows, looking pleased about this hunting opportunity.

"This'll be so much fun!"

Jessica turned to the woman next to her and smiled, then she looked at the obstacle course in front of her. Yes, she was determined to have fun tonight.

Ten minutes later, Jessica realized she'd been wrong. She'd completely failed at the obstacle course.

She wasn't all that competitive, but she was pretty certain that any nice dom would have waited to shoot her until after she'd crossed the first obstacle. Instead, Master Benjamin had shot her ass as she was crawling underneath the first spanking bench. Not the second or third. No, he'd shot her trying to get past the very first obstacle. And now he was leading her upstairs, not even waiting for the others to finish the game.

When she'd tried to protest, he'd just looked at her and said, "I have one hour with you, little one. I'm not wasting it on an obstacle course, no matter how cute you look trying to crawl on the dungeon floor. If I want you crawling, I'll make sure you'll crawl to my feet."

It was the hottest and most infuriating thing anyone had said to her in a long time.

Most experienced doms in the club didn't ask her to scene anymore. When she'd first opened the club she'd scened more often, as had been her plan, but when she'd pulled away after a scene or two, most of the doms had figured that she wasn't interested in a more long-term arrangement with them, and they'd started seeing her solely as the owner of the club, not an available submissive.

It also didn't help that she'd had to revoke a few memberships in the beginning, when her selection process for new admissions had not yet been as refined as it was now. It had left some of the newer doms in the club intimidated, worried about making a mistake with her and losing their memberships. The rumor mill ensured that even two years after opening the club, new members quickly learned the gossip about her. Jessica knew she had no one to blame for this other than herself, but that didn't help her now.

Master Benjamin, on the other hand, obviously cared very little about her role as owner and his temporary boss. Upstairs, he led her to a vacant play area in the back corner. Jessica searched the room until she spotted Vivienne with her submissive Sebastian standing near the front of the roped off areas. When their eyes met, she glowered at her friend in the most threatening way she could manage and was met by Vivienne's amused grin and thumbs up. They would most definitely have to have a conversation.

"Kneel here," Master Benjamin ordered as he put a blanket on the ground right next to a bondage table. The table was one of the first pieces she'd bought for Club B. It had been when she'd imagined that eventually she'd find herself a dom and get to play on it regularly, instead of watching other people use it each weekend while she worked the dungeon monitor shifts.

Lowering her eyes, she sank to her knees, spreading them to shoulder width, and placed her hands, palms up, on her knees. She straightened her back and calmed her breathing down, feeling her heart beating in her chest. She enjoyed bondage, loved it even. Yes, tonight she'd get to enjoy herself.

After a moment of just kneeling there, she could feel herself sink into that head-space that came before a scene. Anticipation, excitement, calm. It wasn't as all-consuming as it had been when she'd been younger, but it was enough to make her muscles relax and her shoulders ease down just a bit more.

"You're exquisite, Jessica. I enjoy seeing you so at peace." Benjamin's voice was a low timbre that made her heartbeat pick up again, but not in a bad way. No, it called her to life, to be present in the way that would allow her to lose herself if the dom she was with did a good job.

"Now, I want you to take my hand and rise. Then you'll lie down on the table, face up. Do you understand?"

She nodded, before remembering to give verbal confirmation. "I understand. Thank you, sir."

"Do it then." His voice was gentle. She took his hand and allowed him to pull her up. Sliding onto the bondage table the noises of the club tried to intrude on her calm but when she felt her back against the cool leather and

Master Benjamin stepped up next to her, blocking her view of anything but him, she eased back into that calm place she loved so much and rarely got to experience.

"Jessica, since we've never played together before, I want you to use red as your safe word. Do you feel comfortable with that?"

"I do, yes. I always use red and yellow."

"Are there any medical concerns or hard limits I should know about? I don't intend to do any impact or anal play, so you don't need to worry about those."

"No blood, permanent marks, or humiliation, sir."

"Are you okay with penetration?"

She knew another blush was coloring her cheeks, and she answered quickly so he wouldn't notice. "I am."

"Very good. If something comes up you forgot to mention, please use yellow so we can adjust." When she nodded, he smiled, and that smile made her insides grow warmer.

"I do like the way you blush," he murmured, before his expression turned more intense. "Let's get started then." He pulled a strap over her upper body, just below her breasts. Then he attached her hands and wrists to the table, before adding another belt right over her lower belly.

"Very pretty, little one." He ran his hands over her belly, first stroking than circling, forcing her attention to her middle.

When she was fully absorbed in the gentle touch, he moved higher, tracing his fingers in big circles around her breasts before slowly drawing the circles closer. Each movement brought his fingers closer to her nipples, but never quite touching her sensitive nubs. It was the perfect torture, constant anticipation without the reward.

Then finally, he stroked over her areola and she wanted to arch up. Instead of lifting off the table, she felt the restraints hold her down. She sank deeper into that calm space, where all she needed to do was feel.

Benjamin watched Jessica buck up against the restraints. The little submissive truly was a beauty. Despite his own size, he enjoyed small women with their fragile looks and delicate bodies. Right now, he could tell she was relaxing into the right mindset, and it was time to up her feeling of being controlled. She responded beautifully to his attentions, and a plan for their scene was forming in his mind.

Since this was a somewhat spontaneous scene and he hadn't had the time to lay everything out, he'd dropped his toy bag right next to the table. Now he could reach things with relative ease.

He reached down, leaving his other hand cupping Jessica's breast to reaffirm he was still keeping charge of her. Pulling out an eye mask, he secured it over Jessica's eyes. Her only reaction was a momentary speeding up of her breathing. Good, she didn't mind having her sense of sight taken away from her. He'd noticed how she had looked around when they'd gotten upstairs, and he didn't want her to get side-tracked by anything else going on.

When he reached into his toy bag again, he pulled out two small pouches. From one, he pulled three brushes. One of them was a shaving brush, the second a thicker paint brush. He left the other pouch and the third brush on the table next to Jessica's leg and began stroking her skin with the two brushes he'd chosen, alternating them to ensure she kept getting varying sensations to keep her mind focused.

When he'd moved over almost all parts of her body, he finally returned to her perky breasts, repeating the pattern his fingers had drawn earlier with the soft shaving brush. By now, Jessica was breathing rhythmically and her muscles were completely relaxed, just like he wanted her. He quickly picked up the third brush and then ran the toothbrush over her breasts, the friction more intense than anything he'd done thus far. She pulled in a breath, before letting out a whine so needy, his erection pushed painfully against his zipped up pants.

Picking the shaving brush up again, he stroked his way down to her mound, running the soft bristles down her folds. Some of her juices had run onto her outer lips, and the sight made him want to lean down and run his tongue over them. Reeling his instinct in with some effort, he continued to circle and tease her with the soft brush, before he spread her lips and used the smaller paint brush to tease her folds from the inside, making sure to avoid her clit.

Jessica was moving her head from side to side now, lost in the sensation, and he knew she'd need more contact soon to reach a climax. He dropped the brushes and lowered his mouth onto her clit, sucking softly. Her scream sounded almost immediately and he could feel her body shudder under him, contained by the restraints that kept her in place.

He used one finger to push inside her, stroking her gently as he licked around her clit. He could feel her contract around his finger, seeking more friction, so he pushed another finger in and continued his movements.

When she seemed to relax into the sensation instead of building new tension, he lifted his head, continuing the movement of his fingers inside of her. With his other hand, Benjamin reached into the second small pouch that held the snakebite kit he'd bought at a camping supply store. The kit came with a little extractor and a variety of different sized little suction cups. Luckily, one of the cups was already attached.

He put the extractor down on the table and pulled his fingers from Jessica's pussy, using both his hands to quickly undo her restraints. Then, he moved her down the table until her butt was on the edge. She stirred, no longer feeling the control he'd asserted through the bondage, so he quickly replaced the lowest restraint to keep her upper body down. Immediately, she settled.

Before he undid his pants, he placed his mouth back on her pussy and worked her until he could feel her tense under him again. Not letting her come, he undid his pants and rolled on a condom. When he pressed the tip of his cock into her slick folds, he clenched his teeth. She felt so damn hot and swollen around him it made him want to drive in hard, but he knew she was probably sensitive from coming earlier.

He inched in slowly, her moaning the reward for his self-control. When he was settled all the way inside of her, he pumped in and out a few times, giving them both the pleasure they'd been waiting for.

When he stopped, she whined again, and he had to grin. Fuck, she was a turn on. Ignoring her incoherent pleas for him to move, he picked up the extractor again and placed the little suction cup over her clit. Jessica froze, making him want to laugh. Before her mind could make sense of what he'd placed on her, he started to pull the plunger back slightly, drawing the sensitive flesh of her clit into the suction cup at the same time as he started to move in and out of her again.

Jessica didn't know what he'd put on her, but it felt as if he were sucking on her at the same time as his strokes were growing harder and faster. At first she'd thought he was about to put a clamp on her clit, but now she was past caring. Whatever he'd done, it made her nerves scream for her attention, and she could do nothing but feel.

He'd reached down to hold her arms in place, not leaving her any room to move away from the onslaught of pleasure. He drove her higher and higher until a pulsing began deep in her core, the waves growing and growing until they washed over her.

When she was just regaining her awareness, Benjamin began hammering into her. He let go of her arms and moved the thing on her clit. The movement was painful and pleasurable all at once. When he pulled the thing off her, blood rushed through her swollen flesh and the sensation, tingling and stinging, sent her right back over the precipice.

She was faintly aware when he pulled out of her and put away his toys, her legs dangling from the table some-what uncomfortably. When he stepped back to her, he opened the restraint and lifted her into his arms. A little while later, she noticed that she was wrapped in a soft blanket and a water bottle was being pressed against her lips. She sucked down a few gulps, the water nice and cool as it ran down her throat.

When she opened her eyes next, she was still being held. She felt small, wrapped up in the muscular body that surrounded her. It felt nice at first, but then more and more of the surrounding noises intruded on her happy place. There were people chatting and laughing, people moaning, and the sound of someone being spanked. And she was in someone's arms and couldn't quite tell how long she'd been there.

A nervous feeling started to stir in her. She hadn't remained vigilant, had let go of her awareness. Had been so drawn into a scene that she'd stopped paying attention. She sat up, pushing herself off the lap until she sat next to the dom she'd been with.

Benjamin. Her newest club member and dungeon monitor for the night. The party was still going on, people were dressed up and having fun. Her head swiveled to take in everything and reaffirm where she was.

"Jessica, are you okay?" His voice was gentle. He hadn't held onto her when she'd pushed off his lap, giving her space to collect her thoughts. The wave of gratefulness she felt was surprising. Many doms tried to remain in control after a scene and she'd snapped at a few as a result. This was better, less stressful.

"Hmmhmm," she murmured, not quite ready for words. It had been a while since she'd gone so deep into subspace, and she didn't really understand what had been different about this scene. The intensity level had been relatively low, but somehow Benjamin had made her slide into that headspace faster than she was usually able to.

Jessica slid a little further back, widening the small gap between their bodies. They were on one of the sofas that stood in nooks between the scene areas, and right now, she needed to gain some distance.

After a few minutes of her remaining silent, Jessica shook her head as if trying to pull herself together and gave him a tight smile. "Thank you for the scene."

She was being perfectly polite, but something about her smile bothered him, just like her immediate retreat had bothered him when she'd come by after the scene. She'd slid off his lap and had retreated even further until none of their body parts had been touching.

Her expression now looked so different from the way she'd looked during and even before their scene. To be sure, she hadn't exactly jumped at the opportunity to spend time with him when he'd first come down to the dungeon, but once she'd agreed, he'd gotten the impression she'd felt relaxed. It'd been obvious that she was both well-trained and in a strange position as a submissive who ran the club, but still she'd submitted beautifully during their scene.

Now she looked like she was thanking him for a good meeting rather than an intimate encounter, ready to move on to the rest of her night. Her smile was friendly, but definitely reserved. If it weren't for her flushed face and naked body under the blanket, it wouldn't look at all as if she'd just allowed him to drive them both into insanely hot orgasms.

Seemed like the little sub was ready to move on from him. Well, he'd see about that.

"You're welcome, little one. Perhaps you'd like to discuss the scene so I can ensure to remember what worked for you and what didn't for next time?" He was fairly sure she'd enjoyed herself well throughout, but as a dom you should never get complacent, and the first approach should always be communication. Given her strange look now, perhaps he'd missed something, and he'd be damned if he didn't find out what, because he definitely wanted a repeat of what they'd done tonight.

"I appreciate that," she said while she got up, clutching the blanket around her. She started gathering her clothes while he watched her. "But it really isn't necessary. I enjoyed the scene a lot."

The words sounded good, but the way she avoided looking at him told him something else. It also told him that any attempt on his part to restrain her and force her to be honest with him right now would only make her retreat faster.

"Is that so?" he asked quietly, keeping his eyes trained on her face. She flinched slightly, before looking at him with a more honest expression.

She stood still for a moment to reply. "It is, but I don't think we are a good fit otherwise, so it seems unnecessary to debrief."

He wanted to laugh at her use of the word debrief, as if this had been some military operation, but her expression stopped him. She was completely serious and didn't that sting. She'd hardly taken any time to get to know him, and, purely based on her own reassurance of having enjoyed their time together, it couldn't have been the scene that put her off him. He wasn't so conceded as to think everyone liked him, but it didn't seem as if she was basing her declaration that they weren't a good fit on much evidence.

Disappointment washed over him. It didn't appear as if Jessica Levington was interested in giving him an honest shot to see who he was. It shouldn't have come as a surprise when not even his own family had been willing to grant him that chance. Why would a woman he hardly knew reward him with her trust?

Clearly, Jessica was all too eager to re-build some barriers between them, if he took her hurried movements to get dressed as an indication. Sure, he could've stopped her from doing it, ordering her to sit down while she explained herself, but he'd wanted her to be comfortable while they talked and some women preferred to be dressed when they didn't know their partner that well yet. He hadn't wanted to push her too much during their first time together. Looked like his considerations had been moot.

"All right, then. Do you need help with anything or should I relieve Mistress Vivienne of her duties and take over as dungeon monitor again?"

"Oh," for a moment she looked startled to have to tell him what to do next, but she quickly rallied. "Yes, please, take over from Vivienne. I'm fine, thank you."

Even though parts of him wanted to shake her and tell her she was being completely unreasonable to just dismiss him like this, he got up and walked away from her. By not giving him the chance to do proper aftercare, he felt as if she'd taken something from him, but he knew when a woman didn't want him anymore and so he walked away.

CHAPTER THREE

On Wednesday evening, Jessica finally put a stop to the tedious task of her administrative duties. She sat in her office with its huge, wood-carved desk and the comfortable seating corner. It was the perfect mix of serious business woman domain and comforting space, which she used to welcome and nurture the members of the club who came to speak with her.

Having an office she loved was also a welcome reminder that while running a bondage club was a rather unusual occupation, she was a successful entrepreneur. Not something she'd ever expected to become when she'd been younger, but something that had given her direction and purpose after her disaster of an engagement to Collin had ended.

Of course, today, she felt closer to a nervous teenager than an accomplished business woman.

She usually kept the worst of the paperwork for Wednesdays, since it meant that she'd have something to look forward to at the end of the day. Saturdays were the busiest day in her club, but Wednesday was the day when the most intense scenes usually happened. While everyone came to mingle on the weekends, many of the seasoned dom/mes of the club knew that Saturdays were a bit too crowded and noisy for the more intricate or edgy scenes. Today, though, the idea of watching others scene was not at all something she was looking forward to.

Master Benjamin would be there and the idea of seeing him scene with someone else made her feel slightly nauseous. Actually, the idea of seeing him at all was making her consider faking a migraine and hiding in her apartment. Their scene had been amazing, and it had been utterly terrifying. And then there was the fact that she'd run afterwards like she did every time a dom actually got her into subspace. Not that that had happened in almost a year. Until Benjamin.

Since her fiancé, she hadn't fallen so deep into subspace. When she'd come by afterward, wrapped in a soft blanket, a drop of water wetting her lip, she'd felt one moment of perfect bliss before reality had crashed down on her. She still couldn't believe how she'd just shooed him off to go back to work afterward, as if all he was to her was another employee, not a Master who'd made her fall apart.

Right now, she wanted nothing more than to avoid seeing him completely. Of course, she had to go into the club, and avoiding him wouldn't do at all, since he was probably completely unphased by her awkwardness and acting weird now would only draw unwanted attention to her.

He would probably be busy looking for a new submissive to play with, anyway. She only hoped that he wouldn't hold her strange behavior against her like some other doms had done. The last thing she wanted was more rumors added to the already brewing mix she knew floated around Club B.

Pushing her office chair back, Jessica stood up. She just needed to get on with it. The worst was probably just happening in her head. If she simply got ready and went into the club, she'd see that it would be just another evening at Club B. Hopefully.

Crossing into the entrance area, she chose the door that led up to her private apartment. When she'd hired a contractor, she'd insisted they build the house to look like the century old homes that were typical for the rural area, except that she'd designed it to be larger, so that she'd have her office and club, as well as her apartment in the same building. Given the hours she spent in the club, it was nice not to have to worry about driving home afterward, and the soundproofing that had cost her a pretty penny meant she didn't get disturbed by any noise from the club when she was upstairs.

When she made it to her apartment, she walked straight to her walk-in closet, opening the doors and scanning the left side that held her fetish wear. It was one advantage of owning Club B. She never missed out on a chance to wear sexy outfits.

Pushing down her feelings of insecurity about Master Benjamin, she went for something bold and proud. Grabbing the red corsage with the matching G-string and nothing else, she dropped the clothes on her bed and undressed.

Even though vanilla people like her tax advisor might find what she did for a living weird, her club members loved what she offered them. A safe place to explore and indulge in their kinks. Here she could express herself freely for who she was. A submissive who loved a good spanking, even if she was still looking for the right dom to put her across his knee.

The large clock on the wall showed nine-thirty. John was probably admitting the first members to the club right now, so she'd better head down quickly.

This morning, she'd put some subtle make-up on, but now she quickly drew a bold line on each eye with her eyeliner and put on the red lipstick that she knew matched the corsage she wore perfectly. There was no time to do her hair, so she just brushed through her curls and let the strands fall down her shoulders, like she did most of the time.

She loved her long mane, and she liked what she saw in the mirror. Maybe she didn't have any boobs to speak of, but the corsage emphasized what little she had nicely. Her bare legs, at least, had a good shape, curtesy of her daily runs. To wish that by the end of the night some tears would have smeared her eye makeup down her cheeks was unrealistic, but at least she'd know she looked sexy the way she was.

When she stepped into the reception area, John looked up from the ID he was holding to give her a smile. "Already looks like it'll be busy in there tonight."

"Thanks John, and don't worry, I have Steven in today, so you're safe from having to help me out." Since Master Benjamin had just stepped in to monitor for the big party, she was still in need of a new dungeon monitor. She'd have to hire someone soon, otherwise she'd be stuck pulling double shifts to make sure the floor was always covered. At least tonight, that was one thing she didn't need to worry about.

"I'm always there when you need me, Ma'am." A former Marine, John always called her Ma'am no matter how often she asked him not to. She might be a submissive, but she was also the owner of the club and his boss.

He had told her the same thing each time she'd asked him to just call her Jessica. *No, can't do, Ma'am. You're my boss here and I won't get my ass whooped for forgetting it.* And that was the crux of her problem.

Owning the club was great, but it also meant staying in her submissive role was damned hard sometimes. John knew she whooped no one's ass. In fact, she'd beg for someone to do it to her, and still, as the owner of Club B she'd landed herself in a position of authority, one she didn't really want on nights she hoped to meet a dom for herself.

All she wanted was to have and offer a safe space for others like herself to explore their fantasies and live this lifestyle in a community setting. Opening this club had made that possible for her. The income from the club was quite nice too, of course. Really, one could never have enough disposable income to spend on fet clothes, but the rest? Well, she'd have to come up with a plan to change how she ran the club in the long run and the first step would be hiring more help once she could get around to properly screening potential hires.

In the meantime, she'd just do her best to make things work the way they were.

Stepping into the club, Jessica soaked up the atmosphere. When she'd designed the inside of the club, she'd used an interior designer who happened to be a domme, and the result was amazing. The walls had the appearance of gritty rock. The material was dark but sparkled slightly. The oval bar allowed people to mingle while watching the upstairs scenes and the dance floor, while the booths along the wall on the right side of the room provided space for more private conversations and pre-scene talks.

To the left of the bar, the real fun stuff happened. There were several scene areas roped off to provide a safe area to swing impact toys and keep people from stepping too close while they watched. Besides a couple of spanking benches, they had a St. Andrew's Cross, and some other bondage set ups, including the bondage table Master Benjamin had chosen last week. The thought made her quickly move her eyes past that particular area.

Next to the last scene areas, a winding staircase led down into the dungeon.

She let her gaze take in the people who'd already entered the club. It was still relatively empty at this early hour, but two couples already claimed spots to play, taking advantage of the equipment that would later have a waiting list. Around the bar, a few members had ordered drinks and Jessica could see the bartender handing out wristbands that showed whether someone had received an alcoholic drink.

She'd vetted all her club members and trusted that each one of them was a responsible practitioner and ethical enough to watch their own limits when drinking and scening, but her number one rule remained. She'd do anything to ensure the safety of anyone wanting to play in Club B and so everyone received a wristband when they had indulged in an alcoholic drink. It served as a friendly reminder to be mindful of overindulging.

Tonight, she could allow herself a cocktail, as she wouldn't need to monitor any of the scenes. Since she'd been struggling to hire an additional dungeon monitor who'd stay on permanently for the weekends, she'd had to step in and take over more shifts herself. It was exhausting to do after long days of administrative work, but tonight Steven was covering the downstairs dungeon and her bar staff monitored the upstairs.

For once, she was free to mingle with her guests and catch up with her friend Vivienne, who had promised to come by later, another reason why she couldn't go upstairs to hide from a particular dom.

"Jessica, hi, do you have a moment?"

Jessica turned to see Melissa, a submissive and new member of the club, looking down at her. It was hardly difficult to be taller than Jessica, but Melissa could easily model with her height, although the submissive's build was sturdy and not willowy like the women who walked on runways.

"Hey Melissa, what's up?" She smiled up at the woman. This was the best part of owning Club B. Melissa had come in a couple weeks ago to finally sign up for a membership after a couple months of being on the waitlist. She'd been in the BDSM scene as a submissive for over a year now, but had wanted to explore some of her riskier urges. Feeling unsafe to do so at random play parties, she'd come to Jessica.

Building the reputation for having the safest place to explore kink in the Greater Toronto Area had been hard work, but after two years, word-of-mouth recommendations were finally paying off and Jessica could do what she'd wanted to from the start. Help others like herself who needed a safe place to live their kinks.

"Well, I was hoping you could vet a play partner for me. I haven't seen him here before and I wanted to make sure he's an okay choice for me."

Part of the membership procedure was that every person who wanted to visit Club B had to give a detailed record of their interests, which helped Jessica make some more educated recommendations about play partners. Thankfully, she was blessed with an amazing memory, a fortunate gift of nature that had helped her go through school and university with very little effort.

"Sure, who is the dom?"

"His name is Robert, and he's sitting over there at the bar. He's been smiling at me a few times, so I thought I may go over to the subby couch and sit near the bar to get his attention. If you think he's fine for me to play with, that is."

Jessica looked over to the bar where Robert was watching them, a smile on his lips. He obviously knew he was being vetted right now and was clearly pleased. His confident smile told Jessica he knew she had no reason to have any hesitation to give her approval. He was a good dom and certainly experienced as well. What he didn't know, though, was that Melissa was unlikely to find that he offered what she was looking for.

"Robert is an exceptional dom. He's a really great guy and many of the submissives here really like him, but he isn't a sadist. He's quite good at what he does, but he definitely prefers mind games over corporal punishments. I don't think he'd be the best choice for you if you're committed to exploring your masochistic streak."

Melissa's face fell slightly. "Oh, okay. Thank you."

After letting the woman stare at the ground for a moment, Jessica touched her arm gently. "Don't worry, you'll find a partner whose kink matches yours, eventually. It takes time to figure out what you want, but if you would like, I can keep my eyes open and make some recommendations along the way."

Melissa's expression brightened. "I'd really appreciate that. Thank you, Jessica."

When the tall woman turned around to head back to a booth where she must have been sitting with some people, Jessica noticed Robert follow her with his eyes, a disappointed expression on his face. He turned his head then, looking back at her. Eyebrows drawn down, he stared at her for a moment, before his features eased into a chagrined expression and then a smile.

Yeah, he was one of the good guys. He'd expected her to give Melissa and him her blessing and be able to play with the attractive woman tonight, not watch her walk away from him. Obviously he was disappointed, but he'd quickly gotten his emotions under control and realized Jessica had a good reason if she'd steered Melissa away from him. She gave him a small, apologetic smile and nodded, making a mental note to introduce Melissa to some better matched play partners next week.

With her first task as club owner accomplished for the evening, she made her way to the other side of the bar where she got a Campari and soda, her usual drink of choice when she didn't share a Margarita pitcher with Vivienne on their girl's nights.

"Hey Jess, did you order me something, too?" Vivienne's voice sounded from behind her, as if sensing Jessica's thoughts.

"Hey Viv, nope, just for myself. You have your own submissive to fetch you drinks."

Vivienne's laugh was full of contentment. "I do, but you're being a brat."

Vivienne turned to the bar. "I'd like a lemon water and a soda, please."

When the barmaid handed over the drinks, Jessica asked, "Do you want to sit in a booth or grab a table here?"

"Let's sit over there." Vivienne gestured to a table near the scene areas. "I'm in the mood to watch some scenes."

When they took their seats, Jessica nodded at Vivienne's water and soda. "You planning a scene with Sebastian tonight?"

Her friend's face lit up the way it always did when she thought about her submissive. They were all but moved in with each other, spending almost every night together as far as Jessica knew, though that didn't seem to diminish their excitement about scening at the club one bit. Jessica suppressed the tiny sliver of envy she felt and focused on being happy for Vivienne.

"Can you believe I've never put him in the stockade yet? It occurred to me the other day when he made me watch some terrible movie about Henri Tudor." The grin on her face told Vivienne that Sebastian was probably busy regretting his choice of movie just about now.

"Where is Sebastian, anyway?"

"He had to help with some fences at the farm today. Apparently, they got some young stallion in for training and he tore down the fence of his pasture to get to the mares. Who can blame the poor horse?"

Jessica couldn't help but snort. "Maybe I need to turn myself into a horse to get some action."

Vivienne raised her eyebrows. "It looked like you got some good action at the party."

"It was a set-up and you better not do that again. I can't even imagine what you said to Master Benjamin to make him come down to the dungeon like that." Not that she hadn't enjoyed the scene. Too much, in fact, but she wasn't about to confide that to Vivienne just yet. Not when her friend needed a reminder not to meddle again, otherwise who knew what trouble she'd get Jessica into?

"Considering how much you nagged me about not scening enough before I found Sebastian, it seems you should take your own advice and get out there. I just send Master Benjamin as a bit of a reminder to indulge sometimes, and it looked like it worked, too." Vivienne's tone was teasing, but Jessica could see the calculating look in her friend's eyes.

"I'm here, aren't I? Wearing a red corsage in a bondage club should be considered the highest level of getting out there," she joked back, matching her response to Vivienne's teasing.

She might talk to Vivienne about just about everything, but she knew better than to ask her friend for help to find a dom for the long-run. Vivienne would be all too eager to get started, as her little stunt at the party had proved. Jessica much preferred to take her time and properly screen the people she was interested in, especially if she wanted to find someone to be with outside of the club, too. If she'd grown a bit too cautious, well, at least she was working on it. Kind of.

Vivienne looked as if she wanted to say something until a loud wail distracted her. They both turned to the closed scene area and Jessica immediately regretted looking.

Master Benjamin had a woman tied to the spanking bench, her naked ass facing the room. From the way it looked, he'd just inserted a large butt plug and was now starting a spanking. The sobs coming from his bottom were a mixture of grunts and moans with the occasional wail when his hand landed on the flat end of the butt plug.

A shiver ran down Jessica's back. She remembered what that hand had felt like on her own ass.

CHAPTER FOUR

B enjamin checked himself before smacking Laura's ass one more time. She wasn't up for the force he usually liked to put into his spankings, and he wasn't a sadist who enjoyed pushing pain boundaries.

He was here to make this a fun night for them both, even if their kinks didn't match up perfectly. That kind of chemistry was hard to find, so right now he just had to watch her muscles and noise closely to measure how far he could take her to make her fall apart.

This scene was a world of a difference from last weekend when he'd scened with Jessica. Despite her strange retreat afterward, he couldn't help remember how she'd responded perfectly to everything he'd done during the scene. There had been very little thinking involved on his part, just instinct. And it had been as hot as it got, even though it had been a very light scene.

His hand connected with Laura's flesh, which had a nice jiggle to it, pulling him back to the moment. This sub was curvy, in a very pleasing way. The way his hand print lingered on her skin definitely made him excited for what he'd planned next. Even though he had her tied down to the spanking bench already, he placed his hand on her back to reinforce that she was under his control. Then he took hold of the butt plug and wiggled it slightly. Her answering moan was that of a woman enjoying herself.

Tracing his hand lower, he parted her drenched lower lips and found her engorged clit, rubbing around it until she got so tense he was sure she'd explode at any moment. Plunging his ring finger into her while his thumb pressed down on her nub of nerves, he pushed her over the edge. Her scream made him smile. They may not be perfectly suited, but pleasuring a beautiful woman was hardly a chore.

He removed his hand from her pussy, grabbing the butt plug. When her orgasm was coming to an end, he pulled the plug out, making her pussy ripple again. He wouldn't have minded plunging himself into her right then, but she hadn't felt comfortable to agree to sex in the club, so he waited for her to calm down while he gently stroked her back. When she'd quieted, he checked her face. She was flushed and her eyes drooped slightly, obviously perfectly content with how the scene had gone.

He removed her restraints and helped her off the bench.

"All right, let's get you settled in so I can clean off the area, okay?"

It would have been nice to get a blow job now, to thank him for the good session so to speak, but with the way she looked, Laura needed aftercare and a good night's rest, not the demands of a needy dom. It had been poor planning but now he had to suck it up and make sure his sub-for-the-night was taken care of.

Grabbing the blanket she'd brought with her, he settled Laura into the armchair closest to their roped off scene area where he could keep an eye on her. He picked up an orange juice and a chocolate bar, offering her both.

"Uhm, just chocolate, please."

"All right, here you go. Do you need anything else before I clean off the area?"

She shook her head and opened the chocolate bar, so he grabbed the disinfectant spray and started to wipe down the bench they'd used. It was a surprise the entire club didn't smell like a hospital with the amount of disinfectant they used around here, but whatever Club B stocked up on actually had a rather pleasant, fresh scent. It didn't quite match the cave like interior, but it definitely beat hospital stink.

When he turned around to store the plastic baggie with the butt plug he'd used in his toy bag, he looked up and saw none other than Jessica watching him.

Unlike Laura, Jessica was a petite woman, but he remembered how soft her skin had felt under his hands. How responsive her nipples had been. She also knew how to dress herself to emphasize all the right parts. Her dark brown curls hung around her face loosely, giving her a slightly mussed look that was sexy as hell, especially as it reminded him of the way she'd looked after she'd orgasmed.

Jessica held his gaze for a moment before blinking and lowering her eyes, her cheeks flushing with embarrassment. Benjamin forced himself to turn away too, focusing on the woman he should be paying attention to right now. The woman who actually wanted to play with him and wasn't running away from him now that their scene had ended.

Laura had finished the chocolate bar and already looked quite alert when he returned to her side.

"Would you like to sit for a bit longer, or go to the bar and order a proper drink?"

She shook her head. "No, I'm feeling pretty good, actually. Would you like me to do something for you right now?" The way her eyes trailed down his torso made it clear what she meant.

The offer was honest and delivered quite nicely. Laura was obviously a sweet woman, and considering he'd thought about getting off just moments earlier, it surprised Benjamin to realize that he didn't feel like taking her up on the invitation.

That was a first.

"Maybe next time, thank you, sweetheart. Right now, I'd like to grab a drink."

Laura's eyebrows rose slightly, but she shrugged and gave him a nod. "I'm feeling good, so lead the way, sir."

Together, they made their way to the bar and Benjamin purposefully positioned himself with his back to the seating area. They chatted as they finished their drinks, and Benjamin couldn't help but wonder what had gotten into him to refuse Laura's offer.

Finishing her drink, Laura put her glass down on the counter and gave him an apologetic smile. "I think it's time for me to head home. I enjoyed our time. If you'd ever want to repeat it, I would like that, and I'd be happy to reciprocate."

He leaned in to kiss her cheek. "Take care, pet. Drive safe."

It was just approaching eleven in the evening, still relatively early for a Wednesday night at Club B, and he wasn't really in the mood yet to head home. Even though he'd done what he'd come here for, he still felt a little restless. Perhaps he'd watch some of the scenes and get some ideas for the upcoming weekend.

Scening with different women at the club was nice enough, giving him the opportunity to sample a variety of play partners and get to know the submissives in the area, but it just wasn't the same as having a submissive at home to command. As a Master he liked to expand his control, something he couldn't do as long as he didn't find a woman whom he was interested in for a more permanent relationship, but after Victoria had taken off on him, he'd decided to take his time when choosing a new submissive. For now, he'd just have some fun and perhaps try out some new scene ideas.

"Can I get another, please?" He gestured at his beer and the barmaid slid another one over to him, including the wrist band members received for light alcoholic beverages. With a thanks, he pulled the band over his hand and turned to the scene areas to see who was using the stations. Instead, his eyes met Jessica's. She must have been watching him again, because she quickly dropped her gaze, and he could swear she was blushing, though it was hard to tell in the club's light.

He scanned her table. Mistress Vivienne's sub Sebastian had joined the two women, and it looked as if the couple was about to leave the table, probably to head down to the dungeon. That man was a brave guy, being with Mistress Vivienne, though he looked as excited as any happy submissive who was well-matched with their dominant.

Benjamin walked toward them, not entirely sure of his own intentions. It seemed only right to greet the club owner, since she'd obviously noticed him. Plus, despite the uncomfortable end to their scene, he'd still had a good time with her, and the last thing he wanted was for there to be any awkwardness between them. He liked Club B, so he'd better make an effort to make sure he and Jessica were okay.

"Master Benjamin, a pleasure to see you."

Mistress Vivienne gave him an open smile. She'd been one of the first people in Club B to welcome him after his move here. When he'd left L.A., he'd asked his friend Harvey to give him a recommendation to one of the private clubs in the area, and instead of just introducing him via an email to make his admission to a local club possible, Harvey had done him one better. He'd known Jessica had been looking for a dungeon monitor and had made the suggestion that Benjamin help out during last week's party. As a thanks, Jessica had allowed him to skip the long waitlist. It had been the perfect solution to his problem of trying to get an in at the best club the area had to offer.

His role as dungeon monitor last week had also helped him get to know club members like Mistress Vivienne much quicker than he'd have usually done, and it'd apparently reaffirmed his reputation with the local submissives who'd seen him wear a dungeon monitor vest and enforce the safe, sane, and consensual rules of the club, if the number of submissives flirting with him today had been any indication.

Right now, though, there was only one submissive who was drawing his attention, and he wasn't sure this particular woman was all too eager to see him again, even though she'd been the one watching him at the bar.

"Hello Vivienne." He let his eyes flick to Sebastian and raised his eyebrows in question. At Vivienne's smile and nod, he greeted her submissive. "Sebastian, good to see you as well."

"Likewise! I missed your scene, but my Mistress and Jessica said it looked like a good time."

So Jessica had commented on his scene? His eyes flicked to the blushing woman, who had yet to greet him.

Jessica's eyes were averted, but when she felt his gaze on her, she looked up, trying to keep her expression carefully neutral. The color of her cheeks gave her away, though, and he would bet she didn't realize how easy to read she was. He'd only seen her confident expression slip once before in the club, and that had been when they'd done their scene. Even then he hadn't had the chance to admire her vulnerability long. It was a shame too, because he'd been far from done with her.

"Jessica, it is good to see you as well. Have you been successful in hiring someone permanent to help monitor the club?"

"Master Benjamin," she greeted. "No, I haven't made a hiring decision just yet, but I intend to do so within the next couple of weeks. Thank you again for your help at the party." Her color grew even darker, and he suppressed a grin. At least he could be sure she'd been equally affected by their scene.

He tilted his head slightly. "You'll let me know if you require assistance in the meantime?" He really didn't have much spare time, but for some reason he wanted to see how she'd respond, and he figured he could make helping out at Club B work for a few weeks if he had to.

"Thank you for the offer, but I'm okay, really. I'm sure I'll find someone in no time." Jessica sounded confident, though it wasn't lost on him that she, like everyone else in their little group, knew all too well she hadn't had such an easy time finding someone before.

"Well, we'll head down to the dungeon. Our time slot for the stockade is coming up and I intend to make good use of it." The twinkle in Mistress Vivienne's eyes was enough to make Benjamin want to shudder. The things that woman would do to her sub were not something he ever wanted to happen to his junk, that was for sure. But as the old saying went, your kink isn't my kink, but your kink is okay.

He gave her a smile and nod and watched as Sebastian followed his Mistress toward the back staircase, before turning back to Jessica.

"May I?" he gestured to the chair that had recently been vacated by Mistress Vivienne. The reluctant expression that crossed Jessica's face should have been insulting, but somehow amused him.

He dropped into the chair, not waiting for her invitation. Though he certainly would have left if she'd insisted, he doubted she would. She never seemed to turn down anyone of her members that wanted to talk to her. Not that she came across as a pushover, but rather like someone who cared for her community and wanted to make sure everyone felt welcome. He might have only been at the club for a short time, but he'd seen enough to know many of the submissives consulted with Jessica to make sure their play partners were a good match.

"So, what did you think of the scene I did with Laura?" It wasn't as if she could pretend she hadn't watched it, now that Sebastian had already confirmed that part for him. He just wasn't really sure why he was asking her, except that he couldn't help but want to find out more about her interests. If she didn't want to talk about the scene they had done together, perhaps she'd feel differently about a scene she'd just watched him do with someone else. He also couldn't deny that her comment last weekend, that it was 'unnecessary to debrief', had bothered him more than a little.

She was intriguing somehow. From what he'd learned about her in the short time he'd known her, he knew she was smart, caring, accepting, and submissive, but she was also reluctant to give up control. And that was what he wanted. Control. Which is why he couldn't quite help himself but push her to talk to him.

As he watched her now, the renewed flush that crept up her cheeks was adorable. She didn't strike him as someone who should get embarrassed easily. After all, she ran a bondage club and had probably heard and seen even more than most people who were into this lifestyle. So what was it that had her embarrassed if it wasn't the anal play she'd seen him do?

"It appears that Laura enjoyed her time with you." Her voice was the same as always, showing none of the same signs of being affected by his question that her skin did. She might be a small woman, but her voice was full-bodied and confident. If the bondage club business hadn't been going so obviously well, she could have quite the career in phone sex.

"I was pleased with how it went as well." He let the sentence hang in the air for a moment, before asking, "What about you Jessica, have you enjoyed yourself tonight?"

The flush on her cheeks increased. "I haven't played tonight, if that is what you mean."

He raised his brows, although in all honesty, he wasn't surprised. After they'd scened together, he'd chatted with a few people, all of whom had confirmed one thing for him. Jessica scened occasionally, but not very often, and she'd scared off her fair share of suitors, even though she still attracted admiring looks. Not that she wasn't liked, she had an excellent reputation as someone who kept her club a safe space and was there for anyone who needed her assistance.

Apparently, despite scening with various doms now and again, she didn't act like the other submissives in the club, and fewer and fewer doms were up for the challenge to get the club owner to actually submit to them. It was strange too, since she'd been beautifully submissive with him, even if she'd used her role as boss to get out of the power dynamic at the very first opportunity.

From what he'd heard, she also wasn't in a relationship at the moment, so chances were she didn't scene in private either, since the rumor mill would be buzzing with excitement otherwise. Sometimes being in a club like this was like being in high school all over.

"And why is that? Why haven't you played tonight, Jessica?" he asked her, not letting her get away with the evasive answer.

She looked flustered that he persisted with this line of questioning, and, like when he'd caught her watching him earlier, he couldn't help but wonder whether she was as unsatisfied by the ending of their scene at the party as he was. But when she answered, she raised her chin and flashed him a defiant look.

"Nothing I've seen tonight has sparked my interest."

The comment bordered on rude, and Benjamin had to suppress a smirk. Who knew Jessica had a bratty streak? This side of her was much more appealing than the frightened mouse she'd turned into after he'd made her come. Nonetheless, it seemed she needed a reminder of who the dom was in this conversation.

"Is that so? Perhaps you lack the necessary experience to know what practices should spark your interest. Maybe one day, when you're willing to surrender more than just your body, someone will show you how good it feels to truly submit. But that would require you to actually discuss your preferences with the dom you're with."

Her appalled expression almost made him grin. Instead, he reigned in his amusement and gave her a stern stare. "Little one, you and I both know that you're submissive, but as long as you run from that, you'll never be able to enjoy the benefits of having this club."

Not waiting for her response, he got up and walked away, the music draining out any sounds she may have made.

CHAPTER FIVE

"Jessica?" Jeffrey Berthington stuck his head into her office. "Can I come in?"

"Sure," she quickly got up to greet her long-time friend. "Sorry, I didn't hear the front door."

"Yes, I noticed." He gave her a disapproving dom stare that made her want to fall on her knees and apologize for being reckless. Instead, she put on her best reassuring smile.

"It's one advantage of living in the country. It's too far out of the way for muggers to pick this place randomly. Plus, I have the video surveillance of the parking lot that lets us monitor for issues outside on club nights, which means I can leave my door unlocked and my friends can surprise me with visits." She gave him the brightest smile she could muster, hoping he'd allow her to get away with it. The trouble with being friends with dominants was that they tended to be slightly overprotective.

"Except your fancy security system didn't notify you I was coming and just about anyone could have walked in here. You don't only have to worry about people breaking in to steal, you also need to watch out for people who aren't okay with what kind of club you run. In the future, you will lock your door, Jessica. Agreed?"

CAUGHT UP IN LOVE

Something inside her loosened, and she let out a breath. Despite it occasionally being a nuisance when her friends went into protective mode, it felt damn good to have a dom look out for her and actually care about her safety and well-being, even if Jeffrey was only a friend. She was so used to taking care of herself, she forgot sometimes that she didn't have to defend every one of her choices all the time. Sometimes, she could just lean on someone. And oh, did she want that. Have someone who she could trust enough to take over for her and take away the added stress she felt every day.

This time when she smiled at Jeffrey, it felt differently. More natural. "I will, thank you for worrying about me. I've been here for over two years now, and I think everyone in the area has gotten used to Club B, but, you're right, I shouldn't be complacent."

"You look like you could use a break. How about you invite me for a coffee and we can talk shop?"

"Of course, I'll get you a cup." She walked over to the coffeemaker in the corner of her office — because caffeine should never be too far away from one's work space — and made them each a cup. Jeffrey sat down in the armchair and nodded his thanks at the cup she placed on the coffee table in front of him.

"Did you come by to bring me the new catalog?" Jeffrey's company produced fetish furniture and almost everything Jessica had purchased in the last years had come from him.

"I did, yes. But I also wanted to invite you to my play party next week."

"Is it already time for one of your famous parties again?" Jeffrey's play parties were extremely popular since he often used them to test out his newest creations. Usually, he announced a party to whoever was around

49

on Saturday and had people come over the following weekend.

"I'll be traveling for a few weeks next month to scope out some new production sites, and since I'll be gone for a bit, I figured I should have a party before I leave."

"Where are you going?"

"Germany, actually. I have some meetings scheduled with a competitor over there who is interested in working out some deal that would allow me to branch out in Europe. It's still early on in the talks, but I want to meet the people in person before I go any further with it."

"You doms and your mind-reading abilities," she joked. "Do you need to look into their eyes to know what they're thinking?"

Jeffrey barked out a laugh. "Don't I wish. It would definitely help during contract negotiations. But seriously, Jessica. You haven't been to one of my parties in ages."

It had been over a year since she'd gone, though she wasn't about to admit that she'd passed up his invitations that often.

"You know how it is. Most of the time, people come as couples to your parties."

"Then bring someone, Jessica. You act as if you don't have any options. You have a club full of dominants looking for a sub. I mean, what are you getting out of having this club if you can't even use it to find someone you're interested in playing with? Besides, you know pretty much everyone who attends my parties so you wouldn't exactly be the odd one out, and don't tell me you think everyone who comes together to one of my parties only scenes with that someone."

His grin was so goofy, Jessica giggled. Jeffrey was one of the most admired doms in the club, but Jessica doubted any of the submissive he'd ever played with would describe the sadist as goofy. Fortunately, he wasn't just a dom in her club, but also her friend. Unfortunately, his words were a stark reminder of what Master Benjamin had said to her last Wednesday. *You and I both know that you're submissive, but as long as you run from that, you'll never be able to enjoy the benefits of having this club.*

"I'll think about it. Now why don't you show me what new evil devices you've invented to torture poor innocent subbies?"

When she walked through the dungeon a few hours later, using her flashlight to check on the scenes, her mind was still mulling over what Jeffrey had said to her. She wanted to attend his parties. All her friends were there, so why couldn't she bring herself to just ask someone to come with her?

If she was serious about finding a dom, she had to bring herself to give them a chance. Except that was the problem, wasn't it?

The whole reason for building Club B had been her desire for a safe place to explore kink. For herself and for others. Well, others were using it and felt comfortable expanding their relationships further from here, but she was stuck relying on her protective bubble. And even that bubble seemed to have shrunk over time. Now she was running doms off after just one scene, and she couldn't even explain why to herself.

She'd done everything in her might to make sure everyone's limits were being respected and enforced.

Only, it hadn't helped her deal with her own fears. She still clung to those, and now that she'd decided she was ready for a new relationship if the right dom came along, it was as if they were worse than before. As if by just thinking about a committed relationship, her mind brought back all the memories of just how wrong things had gone last time.

The irony was, she would love to trust a dom enough to allow him to help her deal with these problems, only the kicker was, she needed to place trust in a dom first to actually give him the chance to even do that. It was a catch-22, and she had maneuvered herself into it all by herself, because she hadn't been careful enough in the past. She had jumped into a relationship and had let her guard down for a manipulative man who'd emotionally worn her down to the point where trusting another man felt like a huge hurdle rather than an exciting adventure.

Unfortunately, being aware of the problem alone wasn't particularly helpful, because even if she wanted to take the next step and actually put herself out there, she now had to overcome the added challenges her reluctance to trust someone had caused. She'd spent the past two years rejecting all the doms who'd shown interest. Sure, she scened with them, but she'd never stuck around long enough for one of them to test her boundaries and help her explore her limits.

She had played it safe. So here she was. She might own a BDSM club with some of the most respected doms in the area as her members, but unlike what Jeffrey thought, she hardly knew any who would still be interested in her.

As she lifted her flashlight to check the hands of a cuffed submissive, she met the dom's nod with one of her own. The brief interaction left her pondering the same problem she hadn't gotten out of her head since Jeffrey had left earlier.

In the club, she had a position of authority, even over the doms, which left her in an awkward spot. At Jeffrey's party, she wouldn't have to worry about checking up on everyone else, and she could fully focus on actually submitting to whoever she was with. It would be the perfect opportunity to put herself out there since all her friends would be around and able to keep an eye on her. She'd feel safe, and maybe the change of environment would help her get into the right head space.

Not that she'd had any problem getting into a submissive head space with Master Benjamin. Except, the second her scene with him had ended and he'd wanted to push on to discuss things, she'd balked. It was the same response she'd had with other men, but this time it had been so much more disappointing and terrifying. The physical submission was one thing, but to open herself up emotionally? Well, that wasn't as easy.

Last week had been different because she'd gotten so deep into sub-space it had ripped her emotions wide open. If he could do that to her, he was so much more dangerous than the others, but it also proved she couldn't stop looking for that same connection. As much as she hated to admit it, Master Benjamin was right. Submitting, to her, meant more than surrendering her body. But she'd still have to be very careful about whom she'd trust with her submission, and to take the first step within a circle of her closest friends at Jeffrey's party seemed like the best plan she'd had in a while.

Now she just needed to decide whether she wanted to ask someone to accompany her or leave things to fate and see who'd show up at the party. Someone who might want to play with her. Really, it wasn't much of a choice, since the thought of not vetting whoever she played with first was not acceptable to her, even if her friends would be around.

Jeffrey visited the other clubs in the Greater Toronto Area to promote his business as well, so he knew people who weren't members at her own club. And that wasn't a risk she was willing to take. It had to be a Club B member who'd gone through her own screening process, which included personal references and health checks. That meant she'd have to figure out which ones of the available doms would give her a chance after she'd shot down just about every one of them after a couple of scenes.

She got to the back corner of the dungeon and checked the two scene areas there. One side of the dungeon held a suspension scene, while the other held a cage where a submissive was sobbing on the floor. Probably a punishment scene. Something felt off, though, and Jessica stopped to look more closely.

At the suspension scene, the dom was busy giving his partner oral, and everything looked good, but when she took in the second scene area, she realized what had been bothering her. The dom wasn't in the scene area at all. Lenard, a dom who'd received a previous note in his record for being less than attentive to his play partners, was standing just outside the roped off area, arguing with a woman.

Jessica headed over to them.

"Hello Lenard," she greeted, keeping her voice neutral. "Is this your submissive in the cage?"

He broke off his argument with the other woman to look at her, his expression showing annoyance. "Yes, and as I was telling Kate here, I'm punishing her for disrespecting me during a scene."

"Except you shouldn't punish Lydia when you set up the scene for us to be bratty. It's supposed to be about funishment, not this..." Kate gestured to the cage.

"I'm the dom, so I make the rules. You both agreed to the scene and I'm not doing anything that she indicated as a hard limit."

"You are, however, doing something that is a hard limit in this club, and that is not monitoring your submissive appropriately." Jessica hadn't taken her eyes off the crying woman in the cage, recognizing her as Lydia, a shy woman who came to the club infrequently.

"Kate, do I understand correctly that you were part of this scene as well?"

"Yes, I was. And this wasn't what we discussed beforehand."

Jessica nodded, turning to look at Kate and Lenard when she spoke. "Right now, what we're going to do is stop this scene. Please open the cage so we can have a discussion about what went wrong here, since there is some general disagreement about this scene."

When she saw Lenard's expression, she knew she should have been more diplomatic. His face was reddening and his chest was heaving from the argument he'd been having with Kate. This wasn't good.

"This is my scene and I haven't heard my sub using her safe word. You have absolutely no right to barge in on my scene. You may think you don't have to submit to any doms in here because you own the place, but if you start fucking with everyone's scenes you might as well close this place down because no self-respecting dom wants to be told what to do by a submissive who doesn't understand how safe words work."

Jessica flicked her eyes to the sub in the cage again. The woman was still curled up in a ball, sobbing. Lydia was apparently so caught up in her own misery, she hadn't noticed an argument was going on. Perhaps the woman was simply deep into a punishment head space, but Jessica didn't know her well enough to know if the woman was even aware enough to use her safe word if she wanted to.

If Lenard had been paying attention to Lydia and if Kate hadn't also been upset, she wouldn't have interrupted, but to leave a sub unsupervised the way he'd done was unacceptable and something about this entire situation was definitely off.

"I understand you're not happy about this, and we can discuss that in my office if you like, but first I insist that you release your sub from the cage. If she agrees, you can continue your scene on another day, but right now I do not feel comfortable letting you continue."

For a moment it looked as if Lenard wasn't going to respond at all, but then he shook his head and his face turned ugly. "This is bullshit." He grabbed Kate's hand and yanked her forward as he turned to the cage.

"Red. Red, red, red." Kate's voice was strong and loud, calling out her safe word.

Jessica stepped forward to intervene and took hold of Lenard's wrist. He swung around and pulled his arm up, inadvertently hitting her squarely in the jaw. Pain shot through her and she stumbled back.

"Someone get John down here right now," she managed to press out. Jessica wondered briefly how long it would take the security guard to get from the reception area down here, when she felt someone step up next to her.

"Stop right there."

She knew that voice. It was Master Benjamin, and his presence made her calm down enough to focus on her next steps. Still clutching her face, Jessica ignored Lenard and took Kate's hand, pulling her back. When Kate was a safe distance from Lenard, who was now yelling at Master Benjamin and the various people that had come up to the scene area, Jessica headed for the cage and opened the door.

"Lydia? Can you hear me, Lydia?"

The woman didn't respond, so Jessica gently touched her arm. "Lydia, I need you to focus, okay? The cage is open, so you can come out now. Can you do that for me?"

Behind her, she heard a shuffle and then a grunt. When she turned around, she saw Master Benjamin standing over Lenard, who was now lying on the floor, holding his own jaw much the same way she had done moments earlier.

"Let me," Kate offered, and Jessica made room for her.

"Lydia, it's Kate. Come on, you've got to crawl out on your own, okay? And then I'm taking you home."

Recognizing her friend's voice, Lydia's sobs finally subsided, and she looked up at them.

"Good, good Lydia. Now come on," Kate gently urged her on.

Half an hour later Lydia had calmed down enough to sit in Jessica's office and tell them that she'd had a flashback to being locked into a hotel room with her parents during a vacation when parts of the resort they had visited had burned to the ground. It had taken the fire department a while to evacuate everyone, and she hadn't realized that being in a confined space would bring back memories of that stressful day.

"It's messed up. I can get tied up with cuffs or rope, no problem, but the cage makes me freak out? I mean, it wasn't even that terrifying of a day in the hotel. My parents were there, so it wasn't as if I was alone. And none of us got hurt."

"How old were you?" Jessica asked.

"Maybe eleven or twelve? I don't remember exactly."

"Well, maybe you should speak with someone about it, now that you know it's a trigger for you. And it might be a good idea to add cages and spacial confinements to your limits list while you work through this memory."

"Yeah, I will." Lydia sat on the couch, wrapped in a blanket with her friend Kate by her side. Jessica was glad the woman had someone by her side to support her.

"What will happen to Lenard?" Kate asked. She still looked pissed off and after what she'd told Jessica about the pre-scene agreements and the way Lenard had changed up the script, completely deviating from the fun brat scenario they'd started with, she didn't blame her. Jessica's best bet was that Lenard had his ego bruised by something that had happened during the scene and had reacted badly. It was a red flag that she wouldn't ignore.

"I'm going to terminate his membership here. Everyone can make a mistake, but he had a previous warning, and he wasn't open to me pointing out that he was making a mistake when he neglected to check up on Lydia. Making errors, even if you're learning from them afterward, can be dangerous for people involved in BDSM, but being neglectful and unwilling to further educate and learn is unacceptable."

Lydia's small smile and nod of agreement were making Jessica feel a little better. Jessica's decision obviously pleased the woman, but Jessica couldn't help think that it shouldn't even have come to the confrontation in the first place. Lenard was an idiot, but he'd also proved what Jessica had known for a while. She'd done everything to make Club B the safest club for people to have fun with their kinks, but she obviously couldn't monitor the floor by herself.

Today she'd let her club members down, and that was unacceptable. She needed to hire an additional dungeon monitor as soon as possible.

CHAPTER SIX

B enjamin strolled down to the dungeon to check out the scenes. At least that was what he was telling himself. Only when his eyes landed on Jessica, wearing a white-trimmed vest and holding a flashlight, did he realize he'd been keeping his eyes open for her.

What was it about that woman that fascinated him so much? She wasn't feeling the same draw to him, that much he was sure about, and yet he couldn't help feeling protective of her somehow.

He watched as she checked the scenes and stopped at a corner play area, where a dom seemed to argue with his submissive outside of the roped area. It was only when Jessica pointed her flashlight at the cage behind the dom that he realized a second submissive was locked up there. That wasn't ideal. Benjamin checked the dom again, who was still busy arguing. It was obvious the man wasn't paying any attention to the sub behind him.

Apparently having drawn the same conclusion as him, Jessica stepped up to the dom saying something. Benjamin walked closer, curious to see what Jessica was doing about the situation. When the guy started arguing with her, Benjamin walked toward them, not liking the look on the guy's face.

When he was still a couple meters out, the guy grabbed the submissive he'd been arguing with and turned away from Jessica. When the woman yelled her safe word, Benjamin reacted. He lengthened his strides and arrived next to Jessica just after the guy's arm hit her face.

"Stop right there," he ordered, not surprised when the guy ignored him and tried to storm off, having completely forgotten or not caring that he had a responsibility to the woman still locked up in the cage. And to Jessica, whom he'd inadvertently hurt. Irresponsible idiot.

Benjamin put a hand on the guy's chest, stopping him. "Don't make things worse than they are."

The wanna-be dom looked at him, taking his measure, and Benjamin decided to give him his last chance to make the right choice.

"Screw this." The idiot tried to push past Benjamin, unsurprisingly making the wrong decision. At this point, a crowd had formed around them, everyone looking at the guy disapprovingly. A sub calling out a safe word could happen, but a dom storming off angrily afterward? Now that was a sure way to piss off everyone in this place.

"Yeah, I don't think so."

When the guy swung at him, Benjamin ducked and hit him squarely in the jaw. Karma won every time.

Someone pushed through the crowd and stepped up next to him. "John, it's good to see you." Obviously, the security guard had already been on his way down here before things had gotten out of hand.

"Yeah, saw there was some trouble brewing down here." The way John's eyes stayed on the idiot, Benjamin had a feeling the club's security guard had been keeping a special eye on him through the surveillance system.

"This gentleman would like to leave, but I think he might require an escort out. And Jessica might have a couple of words to say to him."

"If he needs to be escorted out, I suspect she will," John agreed.

Benjamin checked the cage where Jessica and the second submissive had convinced the crying woman to crawl out. The woman looked shaken, and her friend placed a comforting arm around her.

After a moment, Jessica led the two women toward them and turned to John. "Please show Lenard out. I'll get in touch with him about his membership via email."

That had been forty-five minutes ago and now he was sitting at the bar, checking the door that led into the main club room with way too much frequency. Where was Jessica?

No doubt she'd taken the involved submissives to her office to make sure they were okay before they left. Given how shaken the caged one had looked, there was a good chance Jessica wouldn't emerge for quite a while longer. But he still glanced over to the door every few minutes. He just couldn't help himself.

Fifteen minutes later, Benjamin finished his drink and pushed the glass across the bar. "I'm out."

"See you next week," the bartender told him with an inviting smile. Benjamin gave him a tip and headed to the door. In the reception area, he saw John sitting back behind his desk, monitoring the video surveillance.

"Hey," he greeted. "Jessica still with the women?"

"Nah, they left a little while ago, but she's still in there." John nodded to the office door. "Always takes it to heart when something happens in the club. I saw her approach Lenard, so I headed down right away, but it's just no good with me being up here trying to anticipate problems. I can't get down there fast enough, especially on a busy night."

"You did good, but I agree. Jessica needs to step up her security."

No doubt she was beating herself up about that very thought. She would be the type to take this kind of incident and ask herself what she should have done differently. Benjamin realized that was why he couldn't stop himself from feeling protective towards her.

Right from the first day he'd set his foot into Club B, Jessica had made it clear that her primary responsibility in her club was to provide a safe space for consensual, and, sometimes, risk aware kink. And everything he'd witnessed her do since then had been her prioritizing exactly that. A dom had to appreciate that kind of commitment, but it also left him wondering who was looking after her and made sure she was safe.

"This surveillance system of yours, does it monitor all areas of the club?"

John nodded. "Yeah, it does, except the private rooms. Those only have audio and a peephole to check up on people. I have the images of the rest of the club on my screen, but it took me too damn long to get down there when that dom gave Jessica a hard time."

John looked pretty pissed off that he hadn't been able to stop the idiot before he'd caught Jessica in the jaw, accident or no accident. "You know, I've been telling her I can't effectively monitor out here and provide backup for her in there. She needs help, but she's so damn picky about whom she'll hire, so she ends up just doing the work herself and look where that gets us. I'm going to have to talk with her again."

"I was thinking the same thing." Benjamin nodded at her door. "I'll see if she has a moment for me now."

John nodded with a grateful smile. Apparently he didn't mind getting some backup. Clearly, John was a clever man.

Knocking on Jessica's door, Benjamin waited until he heard her call for him to enter.

"Master Benjamin, come in, please." Jessica rose from her desk as he stepped in, and the gesture of respect made him smile, though he couldn't quite suppress the wish to see her kneel for him instead.

"What can I do for you?" she asked and then shook her head. "Actually, allow me to say thank you first. I appreciate your help with Master Lenard. I really wanted to get Lydia out of the cage quickly, so it was good you distracted him until John made it down."

"You're welcome, and that is exactly what I wish to discuss with you. Let's take a seat."

Jessica started walking towards the little seating area near the window, before she realized he was telling her what to do in her own office. She was incredibly easy to read as she hesitated and then decided she might as well do what he'd suggested. As she walked, she gave her head a slight shake, as if telling herself that there was no point in arguing. Even more obvious was her confusion and reluctance when he sat next to her on the love seat instead of choosing the armchair she'd left vacant for him.

"If you're going to tell me I need to hire another dungeon monitor, you don't need to bother. I already know that, believe me. I have two people on staff for the weekdays. They're club members and I completely trust them, but neither can take over weekend shifts because those are the days they want to play themselves. So I'm stuck with only one person on the weekends, and I'm having a hard time finding someone else who actually has a solid reputation for ethical behavior in the scene." Jessica spoke quickly, and based on her agitated state, she'd been mulling the same things over before he'd entered.

"I can hardly hire someone who doesn't understand the ins and outs of what goes on in a BDSM club. I tried hiring from the club members, but I haven't had any luck so far. I've even reached out to the other clubs, but no luck there either. It looks like I might have to hire a security person from outside the scene and actually introduce them to the lifestyle."

The way her face scrunched up and the fact that her hands were balling on the seat cushion beside her told Benjamin what he needed to know. She was more than a little stressed and worried about the situation, and the idea of bringing in an outsider wasn't something she felt comfortable with. Especially if she needed to rely on that person to do a good job reading the various scenes. She had a good reason to feel unsure about bringing in someone unfamiliar with BDSM.

"What worries you more, little one, that you might have to hire someone who isn't pre-vetted within the scene, or that you might have to train them to understand the lifestyle?"

She looked at him with a forlorn expression. "Both?"

"What did you decide to do about Lenard?" He skipped the title the wanna-be dom didn't deserve.

"I've terminated his membership here. He had a prior warning and today was the last straw. He didn't even recognize he'd done something wrong. Maybe another sub wouldn't have panicked in the cage and would've been fine, but that never excuses a dom not checking on his sub. Nor does it justify his outbursts after."

"I completely agree. I'm proud of you for making that decision. You do good by your members."

A slight flush crept up her cheeks, and she looked both surprised and pleased at his compliment. "Thank you, I do my best."

"You do. Which is why you will hire a professional to make sure no further incidents occur on the weekends that would put you or your club members in jeopardy." While her concerns were valid, she had little choice. She needed someone to help out, ideally someone who knew how to take care of themselves if things got out of hand.

Jessica hung her head in resignation. "Yes, I will."

It pleased him to hear her agreement. She wasn't going to go back on her word, because she truly cared about her club and because she was smart enough to know she had no better alternatives. It bugged him, though, that she obviously thought she had no one to help her figure things out.

"Tell me what you need."

Her confused eyes met his. "What do you mean?"

"I mean, you obviously don't feel comfortable hiring a professional, so what is the biggest thing that worries you and how can I help you solve it?"

Her stunned expression annoyed him. She was a submissive with her own club, respected by an incredible number of people in the community, and yet, she apparently didn't realize she could rely on that community to have her back when she needed it.

She also seemed confused by a dominant's desire to listen to her concerns and help her along. He wasn't her Master, and with her obvious reluctance to submit to him beyond one scene, she was probably fine with that, but she should know better than to think a dom would just ignore a submissive in need.

"I... I mean, I'm not sure how to introduce someone to what we do here. I have already looked up reputable security companies and with a bit of squeezing the budget, I can hire someone for the weekends, but how do I explain to someone who isn't used to what we do, what they need to look out for? I mean, telling them to listen for 'red' is obviously not enough."

Benjamin nodded in agreement. It required some education for the person she'd hire, but it truly wasn't as big a hurdle as she seemed to think it was. "If you would like, I'd be happy to help you. I can put in a few weekends to monitor the dungeon with the new hire and explain what they need to look out for. If you simultaneously give them some educational materials, it should go a great length towards making sure the new monitor would be up to speed."

"I couldn't ask you to do that. You've already helped without getting paid when you first got here."

"It was one party, little one, hardly a big ask. And you gave me an immediate membership in exchange, so, in my opinion, you reimbursed me fairly. It was exactly what I needed to help me get to know some like-minded people in the area and in the club. Really, you did me a favor."

Jessica obviously remained unsure. She tried to push herself up, probably to get some space away from him to think, or perhaps to pace the room while she considered her options. Without thinking, he put his hand on her leg, pushing her back down. She yielded, letting herself sink back onto the cushion, and he immediately removed his hand.

"You know you have a reputation for not being very submissive, but that isn't true, little one, is it?"

Jessica's mouth parted, making her look adorably startled. He leaned forward slowly, allowing her time to escape if she wanted to, and, when she didn't pull back, gave her a gentle kiss on her opened lips. Allowing his tongue to sweep over her lower lip, he teased them both before moving back again.

"Let me help you with this. It truly isn't a bother, and I think we'd both feel better if the club is monitored properly."

He got up while she still stared at him, her eyes wide. "What do you say, Jessica?"

"Uh, okay, I mean, yes. Sure."

He allowed himself a pleased smile. "Very good. Hire someone next week and email me so I can meet with you and the new security person before the club opens next weekend. If you have any trouble with choosing whom to hire, call me and I'll help."

With that, he turned and walked out of her office before the little submissive could second guess her decision.

CHAPTER SEVEN

O n Tuesday, Jessica picked up her phone to call Master Benjamin. She'd hired a new monitor for the dungeon, which was an immense relief.

After they'd had the in-person interview yesterday, Jessica felt much better about her choice to find someone through a security company, rather than someone she knew from within the kink community. The only problem was that the new monitor could only start in two weeks, which meant she had to figure out how to staff her club in the meantime.

She needed to put her pride aside and ask for help, something she wasn't particularly comfortable with. Unfortunately, Vivienne hadn't been able to step in and help cover the weekends. Since Master Benjamin had offered his help, he was the logical next candidate to approach. If only she didn't feel so nervous about it.

She really needed to stop psyching herself out. It wasn't as if she was calling him to ask him to do another scene with her. A scene like the one they'd done at the party. The one she'd run away from afterward. Or the unexpected kiss in her office that had left her head spinning.

No, she was calling him to request his help. Help he had offered, so this really shouldn't be a big deal. He'd made it pretty clear he'd say yes if she could only bring herself to ask him. Plus, it wasn't as if she was asking for herself.

No, she was asking to make sure her club members had someone capable of monitoring the dungeon. Not only would she be completely exhausted if she tried to pull a double shift the coming weekends, but after the incident with Lenard, she was certain she just didn't feel confident in her own ability to do the job herself, even if she had the power to kick people out of the club.

With a huff, she hit the green button. The ring tone sounded immediately, so it was too late to chicken out now.

"Hello?" Master Benjamin's voice sounded gruff, and Jessica swallowed.

"Yes, hello, this is Jessica Levingston from Club B. I hope this is an okay time?"

"Jessica." He sounded pleased. "This is fine. What can I do for you? Are you having trouble hiring someone?"

"No, actually, I hired someone yesterday. Even though I found them via the security company, they seemed comfortable with what we do in the club. It's quite the relief."

"That's great. Would you like me to show him around the dungeon this weekend and give him some pointers?"

"I appreciate the offer, but it's actually a woman and she won't be able to start until two weeks from now. She's a veteran and will certainly be able to hold her own." She could picture him realizing that he'd made a hasty assumption about whom she'd hired and couldn't help but smile slightly. He struck her as the type of man who'd take mental note of his mistake and avoid it in the future.

"Okay, well, would you like me to give her a hand when she starts working to introduce her to some of the safety issues she'll need to watch out for? As a former dungeon monitor of yours, so to speak."

It was time to ask him for the favor she needed. Luckily, he seemed willing enough to help. "Well, actually, I was hoping your offer still stands to help this weekend to monitor the club? And perhaps the weekend after as well, until my new monitor can start."

A long pause followed, and she suppressed the urge to babble. Instead, she waited.

"Certainly. I'm happy to help. However, I would like to talk to you about the other weekend. Would you be free for dinner tomorrow?"

"Dinner?" She knew she sounded shocked, but this was definitely not what she'd expected. "Why dinner?"

His gruff laugh made her think of the way his eyes crinkled when he grinned. "Well, I eat it every day and I like to think that conversations are more relaxed over a meal. Since I have a bit of a drive to your place, it would be impractical to come during the day, so dinner is the most logical choice."

"But why do you need to talk to me?" She didn't know why she was arguing, except that she had the sinking feeling that it would be better to spend less, rather than more time with Master Benjamin. Whenever she was near him, all of her usual instinct seemed to trip over themselves. But one meal with him seemed harmless enough, and she needed his help, so rejecting his request seemed like a bad idea.

Another thought struck her. He hadn't made dinner a requirement for his help. At least he hadn't said so outright, but what if he'd meant it that way? Worry bubbled up inside her and she refused to tolerate that feeling. She'd promised herself never to suppress that feeling again.

"If I'm unable to do dinner, will you still be able to help out this weekend?"

When he answered, his voice sounded less warm, though not exactly cold either. "Yes, Jessica. I won't force you to meet me by withholding my help."

Embarrassment made her voice come out small. "I'm sorry, I didn't mean to imply." His voice had definitely sounded flat, and she didn't like it.

"You didn't imply, little one, you were quite straight-forward about it, and it's one reason for why I'd like to speak with you. I feel very at home at Club B, but I cannot help feeling as if you are less comfortable with me there. I'd like to clear the air and make sure we both feel comfortable around each other. That's all."

"Oh no, you're more than welcome in the club," she interrupted him, horrified to think she'd made him feel uncomfortable. And now, on top of that, she'd insulted him when he'd tried to find a casual way to discuss things with her. He didn't deserve that. It was bad enough that she couldn't quite bring herself to open herself up to a new dom, but that she was now pushing them away from her club entirely was not acceptable at all. She needed to be better than that.

Luckily, when Master Benjamin spoke again, his voice was warm. Soothing, almost. "I appreciate that, but I'd still like to get dinner together and chat. It's not a date, so don't worry about that. Just two people with similar interests sharing a meal, because one of them hopes to become a member of the community the other has built. I understand that you have invited me into your club rather quickly, and I'd like to have the chance to show you that I'm a good fit for Club B. Just consider this dinner a chance for you to do the in-person membership interview."

"Okay. I mean, I'd like that." And strangely enough, despite her earlier concerns, she looked forward to going out to dinner with him.

"Very good. I'll pick you up tomorrow night at seven. Good bye, Jessica."

Jessica stood there, her phone still pressed to her ear, even though Master Benjamin had already hung up. It took her a moment to figure out why she was feeling disappointed at the end of the conversation, even though she'd gotten everything she'd hoped out of it. Then it hit her.

Why was she feeling annoyed that he'd emphasized that this wasn't a date?

When she got ready for dinner the next evening, she was still mulling over that question. Why would she want him to treat their dinner as a date? The answer was simple, really.

She knew what he could do to her. After their scene and his kind offer of help, followed by the unforgettable kiss in her office, she'd realized that he had the power to make her want to give him everything she had. Submit. Not just her body this time, but actually submit to him with her mind and soul. Realizing he was kind, and smart, and willing to help made him even more dangerous than simply knowing they had great chemistry in a scene. Because she liked him.

Even though she'd walked away from him before, part of her wanted him to pursue her. To dominate her again.

To make her submit to him, because if he did that, if he could wiggle his way past her defenses, then maybe she'd get what she truly wanted. A dom of her own. If only she were brave enough for that.

At seven, Master Benjamin knocked on the front door, looking amazing in a simple navy blue suit and shirt. He wasn't wearing a tie, and somehow that made her want to giggle. She wouldn't need to worry about some sneaky bondage plan.

"That's a beautiful smile. I'm glad you're in a good mood tonight."

"Thank you." She looked down, not sure what he'd read if he looked into her eyes. All day thoughts of him had consumed her, and now, seeing him in person, she felt silly about the fantasies she'd spun in her mind. She really wished she didn't blush so easily.

"Where are we going?" she asked, trying to focus on something other than how sexy he looked in his suit.

"I reserved a table at the Italian place in town. I hope that sounds good?" his voice was warm and friendly. He wasn't teasing her about blushing, even though she was sure he'd noticed, observant dom he was.

"It's my favorite, actually."

He led her to his car and pulled onto the country road. It was a sunny day, with no clouds in the sky, but Jessica wasn't really interested in the scenery. She looked over to look at Benjamin's profile. When he turned his head to smile at her, his eyes crinkled in a way that made her own mouth turn up. It was hard not to like a smile like that.

Once again distracting herself from her own thoughts, she asked, "How was your day? You work in finance, right?"

He'd been paying attention to the road again, but at her question, he shot her another smile. "I do, yes. I take care of my clients' financial portfolios. Some of my biggest clients are from Toronto, which is why the move to Canada made sense to me. And my day was good, thank you. I even had the chance to research some furniture for my new house."

"Your house isn't furnished yet? Didn't you bring your things from the States when you moved?"

He grinned. "I did, but I only had a small dungeon room in my old place. My house here is bigger, so I plan on getting some additional items. I'm even thinking about getting some work done to have a suspension area."

Jessica tried to dispel the image of Master Benjamin tying her up with suspension ropes. "Have you met Master Jeffrey? He has a company that makes custom fetish furniture and helps set up full dungeon rooms. His company is called Berthington Pleasure Builds. Most of the pieces I have in Club B are from him. The quality is amazing, and he gives good prices too. You should talk to him."

This time he grinned at her, making him look roguish, and heat pooled in her belly. Maybe talking about fetish furniture wasn't the best conversation topic if she wanted to make it through the entire dinner without embarrassing herself by blurting out how hot he was. That would probably be even more awkward than her conversation about ginger roots with Mr. Garris.

"I appreciate the tip. I'll do that. I think I've chatted with him once already, but I'll have to look up his website so I can ask him some questions about his business next time I see him."

They pulled into the parking lot of the little Italian place.

When they entered the restaurant, the hostess' eyes widened briefly before she looked down to pick up two menus, taking longer than seemed necessary. Jessica suppressed a sigh. It looked like the young girl was new at the restaurant, but she clearly knew who Jessica was.

"Hello, we have a reservation for Benjamin Hoffinger."

"Uh, hello. Follow me please," the girl said, without meeting their eyes.

Master Benjamin gave her a surprised look, but then followed the hostess to a corner table.

"Your server will be right with you," the girl murmured before retreating quickly.

"Am I missing something, or was she acting a tad strange?"

Jessica gave him a rueful smile. "It doesn't happen that often anymore, but some people still react awkwardly when they first meet the infamous owner of the local bondage club."

His mouth opened slightly before he chuckled. "I hadn't considered how everyone around here probably knows what kind of club you have. I suppose in the city you might get away with only your immediate neighbors knowing, but I take it the more rural it gets, the wider news travels."

"Yes, you could say that."

His expression got more serious as he leaned toward her. "Does it bother you?"

"That people treat me like I should wear a scarlet red A on my clothes?" Jessica laughed. "Well, it was a bit exasperating at first, but it's gotten less and less frequent. These days, most people don't bother whispering anymore."

Shrugging, Jessica continued. "Really, I don't care what others think about my club or what I do, but I want to be part of the community here, so I decided right from the start to put myself out there. It means having to endure some awkwardness now and then, but the alternative is hiding in my house and not being able to benefit from the advantages of small town living, so I rather deal with the occasional blushing teen hostess."

The admiration in his eyes made Jessica want to avert her gaze, but he reached over the table to hold her chin. "You're an impressive woman, Jessica Levington."

A prickle ran down her skin, but his hand held her face in place, so she kept looking into Master Benjamin's eyes. It felt nice to know he approved. It had been hard, but she was proud of herself for standing up for who she was and what she did. Too many people weren't in a position to risk their reputations the way she had.

A small cough broke the moment, and Master Benjamin let go of her chin. They both turned to see a server Jessica knew well stand at their table. The woman was forty-something years-old and was one of the few people who'd hardly blinked an eye at Jessica when she'd first moved here. As a result, Jessica liked her immensely.

"Jessica, it's nice to see you again. What can I get you to drink?"

"Hello Marlene. A white wine for me would be lovely. Benjamin?" she asked, happy to have caught herself just in time from calling him Master Benjamin. Even Marlene would have probably reacted to that blunder.

"I'll have a coke, please," he said, and Marlene went off to the kitchen.

For a while they studied the menus, even though Jessica knew exactly what she would eat. Today she needed comfort food, because her nerves were on edge. With the way her mind kept flashing back to what it'd been like to feel him touch her, she wasn't sure she was ready to discuss Master Benjamin's concerns about her awkwardness around him. Surely he'd be able to tell what she was thinking if she kept blushing like an innocent schoolgirl.

When he still didn't start talking, she put her menu down and slid around her seat, trying to get comfortable, her eyes trailing the pattern of the wooden tabletop. He wasn't actually expecting her to pretend she was conducting a pre-membership interview, was he? Not after what they'd already done together. She was hardly in a position to doubt that he was an excellent dominant.

When she finally looked up at him to determine whether she should just say something, anything, to get them started, he was already looking at her.

"As I said, I wanted to discuss whether there is something that makes you feel uncomfortable with me. I fully respect if you choose not to want to scene with me, of course, but I thought we had good chemistry, and I was a bit surprised at your quick decision that we weren't a good match afterward."

Talk about being straight forward. Heat rushed to her face, and she wasn't sure whether it was the embarrassment of being called out on her childish behavior or whether it was because the memory of their playtime together sent an equal amount of heat to a different place in her body. She'd known this was going to happen. It was probably best if she just resigned herself to the fact that she'd turn red like a beacon whenever he was around.

They most definitely had gotten along extremely well in that scene. Only the more she thought about it, the more she was sure that that had been the problem. He'd taken charge of her body so easily, it wouldn't have taken much for her to allow him into her mind as well. In fact, he *had* taken over that too, making her float high into subspace.

She was certain she'd do anything to experience that feeling again. As much as she wanted to finally trust a dom, she didn't think she was ready for something so overwhelming beyond the confines of play. She wanted him physically, but she couldn't trust that feeling alone. She needed to keep her head on straight when choosing her partners, that much she knew.

He might feel comfortable addressing their relationship so directly, but for her to tell him she had an entire closet full of hang-ups wasn't exactly the most appealing prospect. But she was an adult, and he deserved an honest answer. After all, he'd done nothing wrong. In fact, he was being too good as a dom and too kind as a person. It was making it difficult to guard herself, and that was damn scary, but if she ever wanted to get beyond her issues, she needed to give it her best shot. They could be friends at the very least.

"You're right. I acted immature. When we did our scene, I enjoyed myself a lot." She was pretty sure she blushed even more. It truly was ridiculous, given she owned a damn BDSM club and shouldn't need to get all flushed by the mere memory of a scene. His responding grin didn't help either.

"Anyway, it's simply that I have a reason to be careful about whom to place my trust into. I haven't been the best judge of character in the past. Unfortunately, it appears that instead of being smartly cautious like I should be, I've been rude. I didn't mean to imply that I have a problem with you. It's just that I'm still working on figuring out how to choose what I feel comfortable with as I try to overcome some hang-ups that I'm unfortunately carrying around with me."

There, she'd told him the complete truth, and now that it was out, she felt somehow relieved she'd shared it with someone.

Master Benjamin nodded slowly. "That must be exhausting."

There was no judgment in his voice. No questions about her past, or for more details. Just a statement filled with compassion. It helped her continue to tell him what he deserved to hear.

"When we were together at the party, it was the first time in a long while that I allowed myself to really let go in a scene. To sink into subspace completely and without reservation. It was amazing, and it was a bit scary too. I think I was finally ready to make myself vulnerable again," she confessed, trying not to let the intensity of his gaze distract her.

"It's a longer story, really, but I'd had a talk with a friend about needing to trust submissives to be honest with their dominants a few weeks earlier, and it made me realize that I hadn't even been honest with myself, not to mention the doms I was scening with. If I need submission to feel fulfilled, then I was the only one standing in my way. But after that scene we did... Well, I think I fell back into my pattern of only relying on myself."

It was the most honest she'd been with anyone, including herself, and she looked up at Master Benjamin to see his reaction. A smile made his eyes crinkle again, and he reached for her hand.

"Thank you for your honesty. I am glad I didn't do something to offend you that day. I quite enjoy your company and your honesty is a testament to your own strength in addressing your issues." And with those few words and the gentle tug of his hand as he pulled hers towards the middle of the table, Jessica felt herself sink into the strength he seemed to lend out.

Perhaps he thought her strong, but he'd been right. It was exhausting.

CHAPTER EIGHT

B enjamin noted with some satisfaction that Jessica's small hand curled around his on the table. He'd turned his hand so that hers was on top. His fingers gently wrapped around hers, letting her know he was there to support her, but she could easily remove her hand if she wished. Instead, she leaned further forward, as if settling into the new position.

It pleased him immensely.

Perhaps he'd been wrong about her reaction to their scene. He'd assumed that she wasn't willing to commit to actually submitting to a dom. It'd seemed to fit with what he'd heard about her in the club. Instead, here was a woman so committed to the lifestyle and her place in it that she stood up for her kinky community and created a safe space for them to play despite the judgment doled out by vanilla folk in her neighborhood.

She'd submitted to him so beautifully that day and her retreat afterward had been frustrating, but he should've trusted his instinct instead of allowing himself to be swayed by gossip. She obviously wasn't afraid of her place in the lifestyle. No, she was just trying to overcome some fears, and, as a dom, there was hardly a more interesting challenge than helping a willing submissive overcome her problems.

He slowly moved his thumb over her hand, drawing a slow circle, watching her face intently. She looked down at her hand as if startled by his touch. She didn't pull her hand back, though, and neither did she look upset. Instead, she looked thoughtful.

"Tell me what you're thinking," he demanded.

"You said this wasn't a date," she said, giving a pointed look at their intertwined hands.

Benjamin liked her direct response. Jessica wasn't a woman who was easily intimidated, which made him feel even more protective about the way she'd been so unsettled about the incident with the wanna-be dom last week.

"It wasn't supposed to be, no, but I'd like to change that. Would you be open to that possibility?"

"You didn't plan this?" She tugged on her hand now, and he let her go. The distrust in her face was unsettling. Had he said something to make her withdraw?

"Are you generally not interested in dating or is the idea of being on a date with me making you look so dismayed?"

Just when she opened her mouth, their server came to the table with the drinks they'd ordered. "Sorry about the wait. We had a bit of a spill in the kitchen and I helped clean up right quick."

"It's not a problem," Jessica told the woman with a forced smile.

"Have you decided what you'd like to eat?"

"I'll have the cheese cannelloni, please," Jessica ordered.

"And for you, sir?"

Benjamin noticed how Jessica's cheeks colored slightly as the server used the honorific. If the innocent use of the word 'sir' in his presence made her flush, he was certain the little one was attracted to him. Though, to be fair, she seemed to blush with a frequency he hadn't witnessed in any woman he'd been with before. It was fun to watch, actually.

"I'll have the lasagna, please."

"Great, I'll be right back with some bread."

When the server had left, Jessica looked up at him with a wry smile. Her change in mood made him tilt his head in question.

"I did it again, didn't I?" she asked.

"Push me away without giving me a reason?" he ventured a guess.

Her laugh was full and loud and matched her personality. "Yes, that." She sighed. "I'm sorry. I hate that I've grown so cynical. And with you, it seems it's worse."

"It sounds like you have a reason for being distrustful. Since I hope I didn't give you that reason, perhaps it would help if you told me what it was. That way my ego will hold up better when you reject me next time," he joked, wanting to keep things light while also trying to figure out what was driving her strange behavior.

"It's the reason why I opened Club B, actually." She leaned forward again, probably to keep the story she was about to tell him private, rather than seeking his nearness. Since the restaurant was busy, no one would be able to overhear her, but he leaned forward as well. Perhaps her confiding in him would not just help him understand her better, but it would also plant a seed of trust and he was really starting to think that he would like for Jessica to trust him.

"I first got introduced to BDSM when I was still quite young. My family comes from money and my brother went to a private college in the States. One summer, he brought a friend home to stay with us in Toronto. I was seventeen at the time and he was nineteen and had just started to dive into the lifestyle. He was my first, and after that, vanilla boys just didn't seem exciting, so once I got to University I really started to explore submission."

Her nostalgic smile told him she'd had a pleasant introduction into kink.

"I dated a few really great doms over the years, but I was still pretty young so I wasn't ready to settle down with anyone. Then, after school, I started working, and I met someone. He was a dom in a club I liked to go to, and he had a pretty good reputation. We started seeing each other, and we had good chemistry. At some point he asked me to marry him and I said yes." Instead of delighted, she looked resigned at the memory. As if it was a part of her past she'd accepted, but wished had been different.

He waited patiently for her to keep talking, curious about what had happened to her engagement. She wasn't married now, he knew that much, but perhaps she got a divorce from her ex.

"I was so happy about it and having fun planning the wedding. Except, my ex started to get controlling. It began slowly, so I hardly noticed. Little things like checking in on me more frequently. I actually liked it." Jessica shook her head, lost in her memory. "That was the messed up part. He'd been checking in with me before too, and to me it seemed like the sign of a caring dom and partner, but then it got more and more frequently."

Jessica took a sip of her wine and Benjamin felt himself feel impatient to hear the rest of the story, so he worked hard to keep his expression relaxed and take a sip of his own drink. The last thing he should do right now was rush her.

"Over time, I realized it was more than the actions of an attentive dom. Or, perhaps not more, but different. He'd changed somehow, and instead of just checking that I was okay, he started to manipulate me emotionally. Making me feel guilty for going places without him. That sort of thing. So, after it got too much, I broke things off with him. It was a really ugly break-up too, because he thought of me as belonging to him. That's when I knew I'd made the right decision to leave him."

Now she looked outright irritated. "Sad, right? That I needed that confirmation and was still second-guessing myself until then. I don't know what happened. Whether he was always like that and I didn't notice earlier, or if he changed and something happened along the way to make him like that. I honestly can't say. Maybe I was just too naïve to see him for what he was right from the start."

Benjamin considered her for a moment. She didn't look sad or even angry now, just really weary. As if she'd asked herself that question too many times already. He was glad she was such an open book to read, allowing her emotions to play across her face.

"You can't control other people's actions. Just your own. And it looks like you did the right thing. Once you realized your ex got obsessive, you got yourself out of that situation. Unfortunately, there are people who hide who they really are from others, and all you can do is react." He knew that all too well himself, and he understood how it left you feeling betrayed. "But, Jessica, if you never give someone else the chance to show you who they really are, you also won't be able to find the person who will truly make you happy."

"I know." Her response carried equal measures of sadness and determination.

Just then, their food arrived and Jessica asked him a bit more about his job and move to the area, obviously wanting to change the topic. He obliged her and they chatted throughout the meal. As he ate and listened to her talk, Benjamin realized how much he enjoyed Jessica's humor and openness. It was rare to have someone be so forthright about their thoughts and fears. Of course, given the rumors about her in Club B, that she wasn't willing to truly submit to any one dom, it appeared she chose whom to open up to carefully. It honored him that she'd obviously chosen to include him in that group.

No one, no matter their sexual preferences, should feel like they had to make themselves vulnerable to just anybody. The beauty of having someone open themselves up to you and eventually submitting was about trust, and trust had to be earned first.

Perhaps Jessica would be willing to take another chance on him tonight, because if she was, he might be able to help her overcome her fears, and that would be an incredible gift.

After dessert, Benjamin led her back to his car. The evening had been amazing and she still couldn't believe she'd told him about her train wreck of an engagement to Collin, but Benjamin was a good listener and under his steady gaze it had felt easy to share. Rationally, she knew that she'd done nothing wrong back then, and yet she still didn't quite trust herself to open up to someone again.

Except she wanted to, and somehow Master Benjamin had made her admit that to him.

It felt freeing somehow. In the same way she loved giving control of her body over to a dom, allowing her to feel pleasure much more intense, she felt as if sharing her story had somehow lightened the burden of dealing with her problems alone. It was a risk, of course. She didn't know him that well, but she could tell that he had the same dominant impulse to help like the men she'd dated before meeting Collin.

She looked over at him from the corners of her eyes. His car smelled faintly like cinnamon, and she wondered whether he enjoyed baked treats while he drove. Somehow, he didn't seem the type to allow crumbs in his vehicle.

"What is it, little one?" he asked, as if sensing her eyes on him. She felt herself smile. She liked that he always called her that. *Little one*. It felt like an endearment, something that reaffirmed her place. Unlike in Club B, where she was sometimes mistakenly called Mistress Jessica. Benjamin managed to make her feel seen with just those two words.

"I was just thinking that it smells like cinnamon in here."

He laughed then, and she turned her head to watch him. "Why is that so funny?"

"Well, it's just that you've uncovered my most shameful secret." He said it with such confidence and without the least bit of embarrassment that she was fairly certain he was exaggerating quite a bit.

"And what secret is that?" She played along.

"It so happens that I enjoy very girly lattes. The cinnamon ones are my favorites."

Now she chuckled as well. "There is no shame in enjoying something sweet and flavorful."

He drove into the Club B parking lot, put the shift into park, and gave her an intense look. "No, there is not."

Unsure what to say next, Jessica looked down to unbuckle herself, but Benjamin's hands pushed hers away. He pressed the button and eased the seatbelt over her.

She knew she was holding her breath, unsure whether she wanted him to run his knuckles over her breasts or not. When he didn't, keeping his hand an inch away from her the entire time, she led out a breath that was equally disappointed and relieved. Benjamin wasn't the type to sneakily try to seduce her. Part of her was disappointed by that knowledge.

When she looked up, he was staring at her.

"Jessica, do you want to get past your fear of submitting to a new dom?"

She nodded before that inner voice that kept holding her back had a chance to raise its concerns.

"Good. Then how about I join you tonight and we do another scene and this time, you won't run away afterward? When we finish our scene, we will sit down and talk about it. Discuss how everything made you feel and give you a chance to ask me questions as well. What do you say?

If she said no, it would be because she was a coward. She was attracted to him and longed for the chance to have his hands on her again. There was no question about that. And she wanted to kick these fears in the butt, so she nodded once more.

"I need you to say it out loud, little one. What do you want to do tonight?"

"I want to scene with you and talk about it afterward."

The crinkles around his eyes when he smiled at her were her first reward of the night, and she had a feeling there was more to come. Being brave didn't feel all that scary when she had Benjamin to guide her through it.

As they entered the club, John got up from behind his desk. "Hey, Jessica. Master Benjamin. The bar staff is setting up just now. Thomas is already here too and ready for his monitoring shift, so we should be a go for the first members to come pretty soon."

"Thanks, John. I'll be in the club. Let me know if there are any issues."

"Actually, Jessica, do you think John could direct the concerns to your staff members for the next hour? If it's something you're needed for, they can surely triage it first?"

He'd asked it as a question, leaving her the final choice, but it had been leading enough to let her know what he wanted. "Oh, uh, yes. Yes, that makes sense. Could you direct any concerns to Thomas first, John?"

John looked between them with a half smile. "Sure can, boss. Have fun." With the last word, his smile turned into a grin and he quickly sat back down behind his desk. Well, honestly. It wasn't as if she never played in the club. Her spending time with a dom hardly warranted any teasing.

"Let's go then." She wanted to get ahead of this, so she didn't feel like she was walking into something she wasn't prepared for.

Benjamin's eyes were turning dark, and she really wasn't all that sure she was ready for whatever he was about to do with her. All evening he'd been easygoing and had acted like a friend. Well, perhaps not easygoing, but like a dominant friend who was interested in her well-being. Of course, he'd flirted a bit, but now, in the club, he was turning into the dom she'd seen that first time they'd scened together and the knowledge was making her skin tingle and heat curl deep inside her belly.

This was a man who didn't make compromises, and right now he wanted all of her. Not just her body, but her mind, too. He wanted her to let go of her worries and trust him, at least for one entire evening.

They stepped into the main club room, and Jessica tried to lead Benjamin to the bar when his hand caught her arm, making her stop. She looked down to where his hand easily circled her upper arm. His skin contrasted against the soft fabric of her navy silk blouse and she realized she was still wearing the clothes she'd been wearing for their dinner, not her usual club wear.

"Oh, I should change," she blurted out, trying to convince herself that it was a valid reason to steal upstairs into her apartment, and not a thinly veiled attempt to hide herself away from potential intimacy with another person.

"Never mind that. You look beautiful the way you are and you won't be wearing clothes for much longer, anyway."

With a small pull, he tucked her away from the bar and headed toward the back of the room. A nervous laugh escaped her as she tried to resist him, just a little, but he just kept moving.

"Benjamin, the bar is over there. Don't you want to sit down for a bit until the first people arrive?"

"It's Master Benjamin when we're in here and no, thank you, I've already sat enough this evening. Right now, I wish to play and as it so happens, I have a willing sub in my reach, so no point in waiting."

Anxiety rushed through her. "But we're alone."

Something in her tone must have registered because he turned around. "Jessica, your bar staff is busy setting up right over there, so we are hardly alone. I assume they are familiar with what to do if you were to call out red?"

He wasn't going to change his mind, and somehow that eased the worry she'd felt. "Yes, they were all hired to both work at the bar and keep an eye on the patrons at the same time. I trust them."

"Great, then take off your heels now and follow me."

She bent down to pull off her shoes, not seeing any reason why she should resist him. He was everything that had drawn her to BDSM when she'd probably been way too young to be introduced to it. He was confident, assertive, attentive, and most importantly, he truly made an effort to understand and get to know her.

All night he'd sneaked personal questions in that she'd only realized when answering were things she rarely shared with someone she hadn't known for a long time. Unlike her ex, Benjamin hadn't judged her answers. Or perhaps he had, but he'd simply listened and made her feel safe to talk and try to view her life and herself through someone else's eyes. And with Benjamin, she'd liked what she'd seen. Unlike Collin's manipulations, Benjamin's questions had made her feel good about herself.

So, barefoot, she followed Benjamin to the St. Andrew's cross.

"Take off all your clothes and fold them neatly over there."

A small giggle escaped her, and she quickly covered her mouth.

"What's so funny?" He said it with a twinkle in his eyes, but his tone told her he still expected an honest answer. Seeing they were about to go into a scene, this didn't seem like a good time to skirt the truth.

"Well, it's as if you knew me well. I'm not the most organized person when it comes to things like laundry or folding clothes. I could probably use the reminder to be tidy more often."

His smile was warm. "That's what good doms do. They don't simply control their subs, they help them be the best person they can be. I like to encourage my submissives to be tidy because it shows respect, and a good scene is dependent on mutual respect."

After that, he turned around, and she quickly got to work, folding her clothes as neatly as she possibly could. When she turned back around, she saw Benjamin standing with a piece of paper in his hand.

"What's that?"

"It's your sign-up sheet for the St. Andrew's cross for the evening. I don't intent to allow anyone to rush us by signing up while we are in our scene. I'll put it back up after we're done. Given you own the place, I figure you deserve to take advantage of the equipment when you choose to use it. It's not as if you do it often, so I doubt anyone will say a word about it."

She stared at him, unsure of what to say.

"What, no questioning my actions this time?" he asked, that twinkle still in his eyes.

"Uh, no, I guess not," she muttered, trying to hide her embarrassment. She had asked him about each decision he'd made since they'd come to the scene area, hadn't she? Well, actually, since they'd walked into the clubroom. But she couldn't see why she shouldn't take advantage of being the owner of the place this once. He was right. She didn't usually take such liberties.

"Don't worry, little one. I don't mind your questions. We're still new to each other and I understand you're a bit out of practice letting go of your control, but right now, I am going to take over. You have your safe words. Other than that, you won't need to worry about any choices for however long our scene will last."

Jessica nodded, not sure what else to say. It wasn't like she never did this, it just felt differently with Benjamin.

Benjamin took hold of both her hands. "Tonight you told me that you've been having trouble getting into scenes and forming relationships with doms because you don't trust yourself to have made a smart decision about who you're with. Is that right?"

It wasn't the words she'd used. In fact, he'd described it so much better than she'd been able to. Before tonight she'd been frustrated about her inability to submit beyond a scene or two with the same dom, especially if that dom brushed against the boundaries of her comfort zone. She could never truly enjoy herself, because she always clung to some semblance of control. It'd seemed clear to her that she just couldn't bear the thought that yet another man would take advantage of her naiveté and try to control aspects of her life she hadn't consented to.

She'd figured being able to let go with a dom during a scene in the club was the first step toward getting back to normal, opening herself up to a new relationship with someone. Now Benjamin had given her something much more precise to identify with. Something much more insightful.

Yes, she was having self-doubts, and didn't that suck? Except her self-doubts were somehow less with him.

"Yes, that's what it is, I suppose," she admitted as much to herself as to him. Only in her own thought did she acknowledge that, for whatever reason, Benjamin put her at ease. She only hoped that this time it would last after their scene as well.

"And you want to change that. That means you need to learn to trust your own choices again." His voice was confident, reassuring.

She nodded. It was exactly what she wanted. She wanted to have what she'd always wanted. She wanted to find a partner who'd be her dominant and partner for life, but first she needed to learn to be a submissive again. A woman who was actually brave enough to get to know someone. A confident and smart woman who gave up control of certain things in order to live her best life possible. In order to enjoy herself again sexually and to have hope for a relationship that involved a true power exchange.

"In the car earlier, you made a choice, right? You felt good about that choice?" His voice was confident, calm, and all she could do was nod.

"We have established that you have your safe word and that you have people here to reinforce it for you, right?" Again, she nodded.

"Now, do you want to proceed and submit to me during this scene and see if your instinct was right to trust me?" A last nod and Benjamin smiled.

"Good, then kneel now."

CHAPTER NINE

With Jessica standing before him, naked, Benjamin could acknowledge that this very situation was what he'd been waiting for ever since she'd sent him away after their first scene. It hadn't been her authority in the club that had bothered him, but the possibility that he'd never be able to feel her again. See her beautiful submission.

He directed her to the St. Andrew's cross, gingerly attaching wrist and ankle cuffs to secure her to the cross. After he'd finished, he ran his fingers under each of the cuffs, checking that they weren't on too tight. After loosening one of the wrist cuff a little, he stepped back to admire her.

She'd pinned her hair into a loose up-do, which left her shoulders and collar bones expose. Refusing to deny himself the pleasure, he stepped closer, running his tongue along each collar bone, before placing a kiss on her lips.

"Last time, we didn't use any impact toys. This time, that will be different. Are there any limits or health considerations I need to know about?"

"No." Her voice came out breathy and he wanted to smile, but kept his expression stern instead, raising only his eyebrows.

"I mean, no, sir."

"Very nice, little one."

Her flush increased, and he ran his knuckles across her breasts to see if he couldn't get her to turn a pretty shade of pink before they started. Since she hadn't minded his laying claim to the St. Andrew's cross, he figured on taking his time with her.

For a while, he focused on her breasts, watching how her perky little nipples grew in size and hardened under his attention. Jessica's eyes were on him the entire time, not noticing how the club slowly filled with the first guests of the night.

He kept his eyes locked with hers as he bent forward and liked across her right nipple. Her breath caught and Benjamin could feel the intense focus of dom space making his senses sharpen, adrenaline pumping through him. This beautiful woman was giving herself to him for his pleasure, as well as her own, and he'd be damned if he didn't make her see that it was a very good idea for her to keep him around afterward, because she was addictive and he wanted to keep tasting her over and over.

Moving to her left breast, he lapped at her while his fingers searched for the sensitive place between her legs. He stroked her gently, slowly increasing his rhythm and pressure as her breathing sped up. When she moaned, he sucked her nipple into his mouth, pushing a finger into her until her moans grew louder.

When he stepped back, she looked perfectly aroused and mussed, her hair messy from rolling her head against her upward extended arms. She was perfection.

He grabbed the flogger he'd laid out while she'd been undressing and swung it a few times through the air, both to see her reaction and to feel its weight before he got started. Her lips parted, anticipation shining in her eyes. Yes, she like being flogged.

When the strands hit her, he could see her eye lose some of their focus. Being bound and aroused, the added element of the flogger was already helping her nicely along the way to subspace. He settled into a nice rhythm that he knew he'd be able to keep up for a while. It didn't take long for her eyes to close and her shoulders to relax. Jessica responded like a dream, and that was where she was floating off to too, her own kinky dreamland.

He kept going for a little while longer, spreading his hits across her body. When she was nicely floating, he put down the flogger and stepped toward her. Her pussy was drenched, and he slipped a finger inside her easily. The pressure in his balls grew to an uncomfortable level, but he pushed his own discomfort aside, placing soft kisses on her lips as he fingered her.

He rubbed his thumb across her clit until he could feel the telltale signs of her pussy constricting around him. Leaning down, he sucked one of her nipples into his mouth. She came with a scream and he let her ride her orgasm out against his hand.

When she sagged in her restraints afterward, he first undid her ankle cuffs and then those around her wrists, catching her as she fell toward him. He sat down with her on the adjacent couch and wrapped a blanket around her. This time, he had a plan for when she came to. This scene wasn't over yet.

When she opened her eyes, she saw Benjamin smiling down at her.

"Here, drink something." He gently pressed a bottle against her lips, and she could taste the lemony flavor of a sports drink.

She tried to sit up and find her bearings, but Benjamin shook his head. "No, little one, we aren't done. You need to do one more thing for me. Can you do that?"

She nodded almost automatically. She wanted him to keep smiling at her like that. Like she was doing everything right. She'd do what he asked, if it meant to stay like this a little while longer. She wanted to please him, like he'd done for her.

"Remember last time we scened, how you sent me away right after, without talking?"

She nodded again, but she didn't want to remember. Didn't want to recall the worries she'd felt.

"You need to know, little one, that I didn't like that, because when I send a sub into subspace, she isn't flying high on those feelings alone. I'm right there with her and talking afterward helps me come down too. It helps me make sure my sub is okay, and that's very important to me. I didn't get that last time."

Sadness and guilt washed over her and, with the gates to her soul wide open after their scene, her eyes filled with tears.

"No, don't cry, sweetheart. It's all right, all you need to do is not walk away. I have you in my arms now, and that makes me happy."

She snuggled closer into him, content to let him hold her. She didn't want to get away from him this time. Tonight, she wanted to stay right where she was.

Only later, when her legs were starting to feel a bit numb, did she feel like she needed to move. Benjamin helped her sit up and quizzed her on what she'd liked and hadn't liked about the scene. Somehow, it was comfortable, just sitting there, his arm around her, talking about how much she'd enjoyed the flogging. Eventually, they both fell silent, but it was the kind of silence that was peaceful and felt perfectly natural.

Jessica watched people move around the club, registering the various faces that nodded in her direction, and contentment filled her. She was part of this wonderful community and she was proud to have created this place for them, especially now that she finally felt like she was part of it again. As if she was finally the submissive she'd longed to be again.

Benjamin made her feel seen and heard. That her self-doubts had not only taken something away from her, but from him too, had made her want to give him even more of herself, but she also knew that she needed to focus on healing herself. That being mindful of her own needs would ultimately help her connect better with her dom.

The lesson Benjamin had taught her was more valuable than anything else she'd ever learned about BDSM.

Eventually, she spotted Jeffrey walking in. She watched as he joined Vivienne and Sebastian at their table, laughing about something Vivienne said in greeting.

"How about we join them?" Master Benjamin suggested to her surprise.

"Are you sure?"

"Of course, I wouldn't have suggested it otherwise." He grinned at her. "After all, I'm in the market for some fetish furniture."

She couldn't help but laugh. He really wasn't someone to hesitate when an opportunity presented itself. "But you didn't research his products yet."

He raised a brow and looked back at the St. Andrew's Cross. "Is that one of his creations?"

When she nodded, his grin grew wider. "Than I believe I researched the quality just now, and I was very pleased with what I saw."

He took her hand and pulled her up from the couch, while she was still sputtering another laugh. She was feeling strangely light and relaxed. She always felt at home in Club B—it had been her refuge from the time she'd opened the club—, but lately it'd felt like she stood apart from her community. The more she'd stopped feeling comfortable about submitting to someone, the more she'd felt like an imposter.

Today, she felt like she was in her place again. A place where she had someone looking out for her. She wasn't just the Club owner responsible to keep everyone else safe and sane, but the woman who had a dom by her side who was intent on helping her see through her own hang-ups.

When they approached the table, Jeffrey noticed them first.

"Master Benjamin, Jessica, it's good to see you both."

Jessica automatically looked up at Benjamin to see how he wanted her to act. It was an instinct she'd picked up when she'd flourished in the scene as a young submissive, and it felt comforting to finally have someone by her side to look to.

"You can speak freely, little one. Our scene is over. You can relax with your friends now."

As she turned back to the table, she noticed a look pass between Jeffrey and Vivienne, and she had to suppress her eye roll. Obviously, they'd done away with subtlety for the evening.

"Sebastian, would you get us all another round of drinks, please? What do you two want?" Vivienne asked in their direction.

"Jessica will have some sparkling water. I'll have a coke."

Vivienne's eyes briefly flitted to Jessica before she turned to Sebastian with a small smile. "I'd like a Margarita, please. You may choose your own drink."

When Sebastian walked away, Benjamin gestured for her to sit in one of the two empty chairs. Then he went to secure another chair and sat down next to her, placing his hand on her leg. It was a casual gesture, but Jessica's blood heated at the possessive undertone of it. Even though he'd declared their scene ended, it obviously didn't mean their evening together was over.

It felt great to have someone by her side, and she wanted to do whatever she could to repay him for what he was doing for her in however small a way she could.

"Jeffrey, it seems you have met Master Benjamin already? I was telling him about your company today."

Before Jeffrey could answer, the hand on her leg tightened slightly, and Benjamin spoke up. "I believe you forgot the proper address for your friend, little one, unless I'm mistaken and he isn't a dominant?"

She knew she was blushing. His possessive gesture had been nice, but to be chastised in front of her friend wasn't something she was used to. Especially because he was right. She'd fallen into the habit of not obliging club protocols because, as the owner, nobody had bothered to call her out on it, except Vivienne occasionally.

She'd hated how far away removed from her submissive role she'd felt, but obviously a lot of it had to do with her own choices. If she wanted to feel like a submissive, she needed to accept the responsibilities that the role brought with it. And one of those responsibilities was to show the proper respect. Apparently, that was something Benjamin took quite seriously.

"I'm sorry. You're right. And I'm sorry, Master Jeffrey. I haven't been paying the proper respect."

Jeffrey nodded at Benjamin, then looked at her. "And I'm sorry as well. As your friend, I didn't mind you calling me by my first name, but as a dominant member of this club, it is my responsibility to help remind club submissives of proper protocol. I failed to do that. I appreciate your reminder, Master Benjamin."

"I do like well-behaved submissives," Vivienne purred, and Jessica shot her friend a look, but Vivienne wasn't even looking at her. Instead, her friend's eyes were glued to Sebastian, who was approaching with a tablet full of glasses. When he placed the one with water in front of her, she realized she was still quite thirsty and drank half the glass in one big gulp. She caught Benjamin's satisfied smile and lowered her eyes.

What was it about a dominant who knew what you needed before you realized it yourself?

"I've had the chance to sample your furniture in the club. It's beautifully crafted. I love the style. Do you primarily do dark wood, or do you offer different styles?"

Jeffrey gave Benjamin a friendly smile. "The furniture I made for Club B is the primary style I create, and definitely the most popular, but I do custom work all the time. Do you have a personal dungeon?"

"I have a room, but I'm looking to buy some additional pieces. I'll probably call you in the next week."

Jeffrey smiled but looked a bit distracted. His eyes fell on her, and Jessica was getting the strange feeling that her friend was thinking about something other than winning a new customer.

When he spoke, Jeffrey confirmed her suspicion. "Actually, I have a party planned for next week. Saturday after next. Perhaps you're interested in coming? I organize these little play parties when I have new designs or pieces that I'm looking to get some reviews for. It would give you the chance to see a variety of my products, some of which differ from what you can find in Club B. It's always quite fun when we get together."

Benjamin looked at her with a quizzical expression. Obviously, he wanted to know how she felt about him going.

She liked that he took her feelings into consideration, though the last thing she wanted to do was come between him and his integration into the local kink community. With someone else, she may have felt overwhelmed, or she may have decided to skip Jeffrey's party once again in order to avoid feeling pushed into a corner, but the idea of Benjamin going to the party made her actually look forward to it more. Perhaps Benjamin would even want to go together and she wouldn't have to worry about asking anyone to come.

"I'll be going as well. I haven't had the chance to attend one of Jeffrey's parties in a while." She hoped she didn't sound too desperate for him to come. On the other hand, she wanted him to know that this was one of the steps she was taking to overcome her hang-ups. She looked at him, trying to convey that it was his presence that was giving her the strength to stop giving in to her doubts and actually commit to putting herself out there again. To work on her self-doubts and trust that there were good doms out there who deserved a chance. Doms like Benjamin.

"Wonderful, I'll have myself a submissive to test some of those furniture pieces then." Benjamin grinned and, where a moment before a warm feeling of happiness had been, Jessica now felt a tingle of excitement course through her.

Vivienne's wide grin and Jeffrey's approving smile were enough encouragement to smile back at Benjamin and give him a decided nod. Yes, she trusted Benjamin enough to do this. And she definitely desired him enough to want to spend another day with him.

CHAPTER TEN

J essica had received a text from Benjamin a couple of days ago, letting her know at what time he'd arrive at Jeffrey's house today. His message had said that she was to meet him here, kneeling by his feet when he arrived. If she did that, he'd consider it her giving consent to spend the evening under his command.

The text alone had made her excited.

Last weekend, he'd kept his promise and monitored the dungeon. Each time he'd passed by her, he'd touched her. Moving a lock of hair from her face, stroking his thumb over her lip, patting her bottom in passing. It'd left her in a constant state of awareness and she'd caught herself passing his path more often than would have been sheer coincidence.

She knew their interactions had drawn the attention of several of her club's patrons, but she'd been too caught up in those stolen moments to have cared about the gossip spreading around like wildfire. In fact, when she'd asked Steven and Thomas, her dungeon monitors who usually worked under the week, to cover this Saturday in exchange for a weekday of their choosing off, they'd both teasingly told her they could hardly say no if the rumors were right that Club B's newest dom was requesting her presence at Jeffrey's party.

It had all worked out rather nicely, and starting next week she had the newest dungeon monitor begin her work at Club B, so Jessica would no longer need to worry about the scheduling so much.

As she sat with her friends, conversations going on around her, she kept watching the door. He should get here any minute and she was certain the waiting was going to be the end of her. She was too nervous to pay any attention to anything that was being said, and Vivienne and the others had given up trying to pull her into their conversation.

She'd arrived early, knowing Vivienne and Sebastian would get there around the same time. Jeffrey lived in a beautiful house with a closed off backyard that bordered on a lake. He'd set up several tables and chairs on the screened-in back deck and had put out a variety of finger sandwiches and hors d'oeuvres.

The drinks were limited to non-alcoholic beverages. Since Jeffrey didn't drink himself, he also preferred not to serve alcohol, which suited Jessica just fine. She preferred it when everyone kept their senses during play parties.

"When are we going to start the game?" someone she didn't know asked from one of the other tables.

"In about fifteen minutes. We're still waiting for a couple more people to arrive from the city."

There were eleven people already there, including their host, and Jeffrey had told them earlier he'd invited thirteen people, which would leave them at an even number for Jeffrey's game. He always came up with a party game to start off the evening before everyone spread out and made use of Jeffrey's enormous basement dungeon as well as the two guest bedrooms.

The doorbell rang and Jeffrey got up to open it. Through the glass doors that separated the deck from the living room, she could see three people enter the house. Jessica jumped to her feet, interrupting Vivienne mid-sentence. Ignoring her friend's confused look, Jessica walked toward the entrance. Jeffrey was just welcoming the couple that had come in first, taking their coats, while Benjamin was waiting patiently behind them.

She gingerly passed by Jeffrey and the couple to come to a halt next to Benjamin. Without hesitation, she sank to her knees. It was her way of telling him she wanted to spend the evening with him, and she'd waited to do this since she'd received his text earlier.

Right now, she didn't want to inspect her eager feelings or worry whether she was being too quick to agree to his invitation, all she wanted was to spend the evening with Benjamin and learn a bit more about him, because the person she'd gotten to know so far was a man she liked more than she dared to admit just yet.

"Ah, little one, I'm very happy to see you," he said, placing his hand gently on her bowed head. "You can stand up now. The floor looks rather hard and I do believe I will get more opportunities this evening to see you kneel for me."

She rose to her feet, leaving her head bowed. Although she'd looked forward to attending this party with him, now that he was here, she felt strangely shy. Had he looked forward to tonight as much as she had? She glanced up at his face and found him watching her.

"We'll discuss that thought later when we have some privacy," Benjamin murmured before he stepped up to greet Jeffrey, leaving her feeling slightly unsettled. Like their last scene, he'd expect her to surrender more than her body tonight, and she dreaded and craved it in equal measures.

"Thank you again for inviting me to your home. I appreciate the opportunity to sample your furniture, but also to get to know you and some others from the area a bit better."

"Happy to have you, especially since it's nice to see our Jessica joining you. Responsible members of Jessica's Club B community who treat their partners with respect are always welcome in my home." The meanings layered in his tone made Jessica want to smile. The warning and reminder that the party tonight was full of people who knew and liked Jessica from Club B wasn't exactly subtle.

It was nice that her friends cared to see her happy, but it felt strange that Jeffrey wanted to put some of that responsibility on Benjamin. Not that he seemed to mind, since his arm tightened around her possessively. It made her feel lighter, as if the happiness that was nervously bubbling in her stomach helped her float just a little.

"It appears Jessica inspires loyalty, and I've witnessed her display that same loyalty to her own friends. I hope to earn that for myself." Benjamin's tone was perfectly calm, but the words caused Jessica's heart to race. She glanced up to see him smile down at her, and the telltale heat of a blush creeped up her neck.

Jeffrey's chuckle thankfully broke the strange tension that had built in the entrance area, and he gestured for them to head out to the screened-in deck where space heaters allowed them to sit with a beautiful view of the lake.

"We'll begin the party game in a few minutes. It's a tradition at my parties and I'll explain the rules before we get started."

Benjamin clasped Jessica's hand and tugged her along.

When they stepped outside, he quickly scanned the tables that were already filled with a number of people, most of them sitting, but some kneeling by their dominants' side. When his eyes met those of Vivienne, the domme smiled and pointed at an empty chair at their table, presumably the place Jessica had sat in before he'd arrived.

He was pleased that she'd come to him right away. He hadn't been sure what the best approach was before, but it seemed his strategy to give Jessica a choice to come to him if she wanted to spend the party with him had worked out. It would have been much less fun if she'd decided that she wasn't willing to allow him to push her further.

She was a brave little one, and he hadn't been this excited to get to know someone in a very long time.

When they reached the table, he took the pillow off the deck chair before he sat down. He put it on the ground next to him and nodded for Jessica to kneel there. They needed to have a conversation about their respective expectations if this evening went well, because if the evening worked out similar to the scenes they'd done thus far, he intended to pursue this connection between them more seriously, and that would require some further discussion.

He wondered whether the little one would be ready for that after her ex had messed with her head so much. She might find the idea to give up as much control as he wanted intimidating, since she wouldn't be able to hang on to her usual defence strategy of pulling back. But she sank down on the pillow with a small smile, her shoulder touching his leg. She was braver than many, and a strange feeling of pride ran through him at the beautiful woman submitting to him.

They did the usual small talk before Jeffrey stepped to the middle of the tables and raised his hands for everyone to quiet down.

"All right everybody, if I could have your attention please? Tonight we are fourteen and it looks like everyone showed up in pairs, so for our game tonight, we'll stick to those couples as our teams. The first task is for the dominants. You'll need to get your sub all hot and bothered before we get started properly. However, no sub is allowed to come. Most of you already know how to get down to my dungeon. Everyone else, just follow the masses and remember to bring your stuff. Please leave your food and drinks behind, we'll get a chance to eat more later. In the meantime, I have bottled water for everyone downstairs."

Benjamin rose, grabbing hold of his toy bag that he'd shoved under the chair, and tapped Jessica's shoulder, telling her to stand up. She reacted immediately, and he loved how responsive she was. If she were his, he'd teach her all the subtle commands he liked to use, but in the meantime he could enjoy how willing she was to listen for his voice to tell her what she was supposed to do.

They followed Vivienne and Sebastian. It seemed that the domme was familiar with Jeffrey's house, while Sebastian was looking around with curiosity, suggesting he was here for the first time as well. They were in the front of the group, so when they headed straight for a large bookshelf in the living space, Benjamin could see

Sebastian giving his Mistress a look that seemed to question whether she knew where the heck she was going. Benjamin eyed the large shelf, and a suspicion made him smile.

Indeed, Vivienne walked right up to the bookshelf and pressed a button on the side. With a click, the shelf swung open an inch. The group made space for Vivienne to open the hidden door.

"Now, this is cool," Sebastian exclaimed, and laughter and agreements came from the rest of the group.

"It's smart," Jessica said. "This way, Jeffrey doesn't have to have uncomfortable conversations about certain guests not being allowed in some areas of his house when they visit. When he expects his family, he hangs a picture frame over the button and no one is the wiser."

Sebastian nodded before turning to follow his Mistress down the staircase that the door had hidden. Benjamin could appreciate both the practical aspects of such a hidden entrance to Jeffrey's dungeon as well as the excitement factor a secret door added, but he couldn't help the bitter feeling in his chest at the thought that such measures were necessary to hide one's interest from family.

Benjamin knew all too well how bad it got when your family discovered your predilections and painted you in the worst colors. There was a reason for why he'd moved away from his home in L.A., after all. Even if the move had been one he'd considered making for a while for his business, the fact remained that it had been his own father and sister that had finally driven him away. That still wasn't an easy pill to swallow.

When they reached the bottom of the stairs, his eyes widened. Jessica sidled up next to him, gingerly taking his hand. He gave her a surprised look. She was being more open to being with him than he had expected, given her own confession about her past reluctance to open herself up to someone new. When he looked at her, though, he caught the concern in her eyes.

Apparently, his thoughts about his family must have shown on his face and the little submissive had wanted to comfort him with her touch. She really was a sweet one. He pressed her hand and pulled it to his lips to place a gentle kiss on it before he turned back to the massive dungeon that must span the entirety of Jeffrey's large home.

Beams stood in regular intervals throughout the basement, and it seemed as if each one of them was outfitted with some sort of bondage set up. In addition, there was probably every single type of BDSM equipment in this dungeon that Benjamin had ever seen or heard of. It was amazing.

"Welcome to my adult playground," Jeffrey laughed as he made his way to the front of the group. "We'll stick to the front of the dungeon for the warmup. After the game, you're all welcome to spread out and try out whichever stations tickle your fancy."

Benjamin grinned. Jeffrey wasn't wrong. This was like a playground, and he was getting very excited to explore.

With a wide gesture, Jeffrey pointed to the right, where a wall held all kinds of wooden paddles, floggers, crops, and whips. "I'll give you all fifteen minutes for warm up. Feel free to use anything you see down here. Submissives, you can place your clothing in one of the cubbies over there." With that, Jeffrey pointed to the opposite wall, where a large shelf held cubby-holes.

Benjamin gave Jessica a nod to let her know she should go and undress, happy when he saw her smile at him. No sign of regretting her choice then. That was good.

Unlike what his family thought of him, he wasn't in the habit of scening with women who weren't absolutely sure they wanted to be there, though with Jessica's request to help her open up again, it also wouldn't have been a surprise to see her push back at some point. It was a careful balance to always maintain consent but also to enforce his command over her choices when she wasn't sure herself that she wanted to do something. Right now, though, it looked like Jessica was sure she wanted to be his for the evening.

He watched briefly as she walked away, but then turned to the wall with implements with growing interest. He might as well take advantage of the offerings. When he walked over, he noted others were already picking up the standard warm up toys like floggers and paddles.

Scanning the other options, his eyes caught on a silver Wartenberg wheel. After a moment's hesitation, he took it from the hook it was on. He had to keep in mind he only had a short time for the warmup, but he could make it work.

Expecting Jessica to come and find him when she was done undressing, he looked over the different bondage set ups near him. He was pretty certain that Jeffrey had more scene areas than Club B. After some contemplation, he decided on a padded table that looked like it had adjustable straps to tie your submissive down. He wouldn't be using those right now, though the reminder of their first scene on the bondage table in Club B might come in handy to help Jessica get into the right headspace faster.

"Master Benjamin." Jessica's voice was low as she drew his attention to her. Instead of looking up into his face, she'd trained her eyes on the shiny Wartenberg wheel in his hand. Her expression told him exactly what she was feeling. Hesitant curiosity with some nervousness mixed in. She really was like an open book.

"Have you ever played with one of these, little one?"

She nodded her head. "Yes, sir."

"And did you like it?"

"Sure, I mean, I didn't mind it, anyway. I'm a bit ticklish though."

He gave her a measured look, taking in the way she was nibbling on the inside of her lip. Lower down, her hands were pressed to her thighs. "Then, tell me, little one, why do you suddenly look nervous? We've played together before and you seemed to look forward to spending the evening together when I arrived."

Her cheeks flushed slightly. "It's just. Well, when I received your references, it said you were not just a dominant but a sadist as well, and I'm not really a masochist."

He couldn't quite hide his grin, and she gave him an annoyed look.

"It's not funny. Those things can draw blood, you know?"

He knew that, of course, but right now he didn't want to waste any time on a discussion about blood play.

"I can reassure you then. I have done some more intense scene with some masochists in the past, and I believe those women left feeling satisfied, but it turns out sadism isn't something that gets me overly excited. I don't mind doling out pain, but I'm definitely a dominant first and foremost, and I'm not looking for masochists to play with. I want a submissive. And since you are my submissive tonight, I want you to hop on this table and lie down on your back. I promise I won't break your skin with the wheel. We'll call it a hard limit. This is only to warm you up and your normal safe words apply."

When she scooted onto the table with her naked butt, she looked mostly reassured. He waited until she was far enough back that both her legs lay straight on the table, then he wrapped his hands around her ankles. "Lie back now. Don't move." Whatever remaining nervousness she felt because of the Wartenberg wheel would make sure she'd hold herself perfectly still.

He began sliding his hands up her legs slowly, squeezing every once in a while. He didn't touch her intimately, but let his hands slide over her hips instead and then upward over her stomach until he reached her breasts. Using his fingers, he drew circles around them, slowly letting the circles get smaller and smaller until he was tracing her areola. The rhythmic moving of her chest stopped, and he almost snorted. Yeah, she was no doubt thinking back to their first scene now.

"Keep breathing, little one."

When she pulled in a breath, he pinched her nipples, making her gasp in response. The look of outrage she shot in his direction made him want to laugh out loud. She was too cute. Instead, he toyed with her nipples, pulling and tugging them until her breathing sped up even more. Finally, he picked up the Wartenberg wheel from where he'd put it on the table and drew it up her upper thighs and back down at a slightly different angle, adjusting his hold to make sure the sensation would be different.

He used his left hand to push her legs apart, allowing him to see her pink pussy. The temptation to touch her was strong, but he focused on moving the wheel up and down her inner thighs, easing up on the pressure he put on it to make sure he didn't break her sensitive skin.

When he stopped just before he reached her pussy, pulling the wheel back down, Jessica let out an adorable moan that was a mix of relief and torture. In response, the next time he pulled the wheel up her leg, he drew it gently across her hipbone and further up, starting a circular pattern around her naval.

When her breathing relaxed again, he let his circles grow bigger, until the wheel almost touched the underside of her breasts. The small mounds didn't create creases like the breasts of fuller women, but her nipples poked up, calling attention to themselves. Instead of completing the circle, Benjamin started a back-and-forth motion, drawing the little toy across the lower side of Jessica's breasts. Her answering moan was beautiful.

The next stroke pulled over the upper side of her breasts, then again across the underside, but slightly closer to her nipples this time. He repeated this pattern, below and above her nipples, constantly getting closer to those perky nubs.

Just before he would have pulled the wheel across her areola, Jessica's breathing stopped again. Benjamin pulled the wheel away and instead placed his open mouth around her right breast. He sucked on her nipple and pressed it against the roof of his mouth with his tongue. Jessica let out a huffed scream and her hands reached for his head. He dropped the Wartenberg wheel to the table and used his hands to restrain her, holding both her wrists over her head.

Then he turned to her left breast, repeating the movement and sucking her nipple into his mouth. Her moan made him want more of her. He had to remind himself that they had all evening before he ravished her completely.

"Turn around and lie on your belly now."

With slightly dazed eyes, Jessica looked at him before his command registered. Once she'd done as he'd asked, he started a light spanking. He didn't know what type of game Jeffrey had come up with, but he might as well be thorough.

Before he could increase the intensity, Jeffrey interrupted them. "All right, it's time for tonight's game to begin. Everyone come gather over here, please."

Benjamin helped Jessica off the table and wrapped his arm around her as they gathered with the rest of the guests. A sense of pride rose in him when he noticed that she leaned against him, allowing him to take some of her weight.

This woman kept impressing him, and he wondered if she knew what she was opening herself up to, because after seeing her fall to her knees to ask for his dominance tonight, he wasn't sure he was willing to let her walk away again.

CHAPTER ELEVEN

H er naked skin felt sensitive as she stood next to Benjamin, waiting for Jeffrey to explain tonight's game. Benjamin's hands and the Wartenberg wheel had made it impossible to think about what he'd said just before they'd started.

I want a submissive.

He hadn't used the plural, no, he'd used the singular. Maybe she was making too much of this, but it had sounded as if he was looking for a submissive for himself, rather than being content playing with various partners at Club B. And tonight, she was that woman. She was the one he was with.

Since her engagement broke off and she'd opened her club, a number of doms had tried to court her after she'd scened with them, but each time their interest in her had felt uncomfortable. Not that she'd disliked them as people, but somehow it had felt as if they were trying to push her to agree to something she wasn't quite ready for.

With Benjamin she felt different, but she wasn't yet prepared to say for certain whether it was the timing or Benjamin himself, who made the difference, though she suspected she knew the answer. Whatever the case, she felt no nagging feeling at the back of her mind second guessing her decision to be with him tonight. Instead, she felt aroused.

"Tonight's game is a card game. We will have three rounds. Each round the teams will each pull a card from this deck." Jeffrey held up a card deck. "The cards will give you a task that you need to accomplish in that round. We'll allow ten minutes for each round of the game. If you complete your task, you advance to the next round. If you didn't succeed, you can choose one team to support instead. When they pull their card for the next round, you can offer them your help in accomplishing the task."

"And what types of tasks are on those cards?" someone asked, but Jeffrey just chuckled, ignoring the question.

"Let's get started, shall we? Dominants, you choose whether you or your submissive will pick the first card. Don't look at your card until I hit the timer to start the round." Jeffrey placed the deck of cards on a table. "Let's go."

"Jessica, please get our card," Master Benjamin said calmly, and she joined six other guests at the table. When she saw the card deck up close, she noticed that each card was decorated with a depiction from the Kama Sutra. She'd have to ask Jeffrey whether he'd had them printed himself.

She'd just made it back to Benjamin's side with their card when Jeffrey called, "Start now."

She flipped the card over and held it so they could both read it together.

Secure a toy on the submissive member of the team.

The toy needs to serve as a leash.

The toy may not be attached to the submissive's arms, legs, or neck.

"Well, that's easy enough," Benjamin said, smiling at her confidently. "We'll ace this round."

He looked much too happy about this first round, if Jessica had any say in the matter. The first thing that came to her mind were nipple clamps, and she wasn't sure she was looking forward to that prospect.

"Come now, we only have five minutes after all."

She wouldn't drag her feet, since that was rarely a good idea when a dom was excited to get somewhere, but Jessica couldn't quite suppress the nervous anxiety rising in her when Benjamin grabbed his toy bag and led her to the same table they'd used minutes earlier.

"Face the table and bend over at your waist. You can relax there while I get your leash secured."

She did as she was told and rested her upper body and head on the table, pressing her breasts against the cool leather of the cushioned surface. She kept her legs close together for now, since the position already exposed her to anyone walking past. With each passing second, her nervousness increased.

The way he'd placed her meant that he wouldn't put nipple clamps on her, which didn't exactly make her feel less anxious, since her butt was high up in the air as if begging for attention, and she very much doubted that that was a coincidence.

"I wonder what we'll be using these leashes for," Benjamin mused behind her. Then his foot nudged her legs apart. "Open up now, little one. I'd be quite disappointed if we'd fail at the first round."

When she'd spread her legs to about shoulder widths apart, he nudged her feet even further. Now he could reach and see everything, and an excited shudder ran down her spine.

"I assume you've done anal play before?"

When she hesitated, he moved closer and pressed himself against her naked ass. His jeans felt rough against her sensitive skin and her insides clenched at the reminder that he was in charge. "I have, yes."

"Wonderful. I'm looking forward to this." With that, he stepped back. "This might be a tad cold now," he warned a second before a cold gel hit her asshole. She jumped slightly and his chuckle made her want to turn around and tell him off, but one of his hands pressed onto her lower back, holding her in place, while his other hand moved to her ass.

His hand grabbed her butt cheek and squeezed slightly before one of his fingers massaged the lube into her ass. His finger dipped into her asshole and all thoughts vanished. When she reflexively tensed her cheeks, he made a warning sound, and she quickly relaxed herself. It was hardly the first time someone had played with her butt and she actually liked it, but it still left her feeling vulnerable, not knowing what he was about to put in her.

His finger dipped in deeper, and soon a second one joined the first. "Hmmm, I'd love to take my time, but as it stands, we'll have to continue this later." He withdrew his fingers, and she wanted to moan at the sensation, but before she could decide whether she missed his touch or was relieved that the intrusion had stopped, something else pressed against her entrance.

"Relax now, Jessica. You know how this works." Instinctively, she responded to his words, relaxing her muscles and pressing back against the butt plug. When it plopped in quickly, she realized that he'd picked a relatively small one.

Benjamin reached forward and flipped something that was attached to the plug. She felt the soft sensation of something furry and when she twisted around, she could see that she had a long, furry black tail.

"Come on, let's get back to the card table. The ten minutes are just about up." In fact, when Jessica straightened, trying to ignore the weird sensation of the butt plug pressing against strange places, Jeffrey's timer went off.

Master Benjamin took hold of her tail and led her back to meet with the rest of Jeffrey's guests. When she fell a step behind, he tugged and the plug pressed against her asshole, making her clench her butt and stumble. He turned to her and raised an eyebrow, so she quickly righted herself and sped up, walking next to him. The satisfied smile on his face told her Benjamin was already liking this game.

When she looked around, she saw Vivienne leading Sebastian by a leather band that was wrapped intricately around his balls and erect shaft. That her friend could do that in such a short time was both impressive and slightly terrifying. When Master Benjamin followed her gaze, he pretended to shudder and she couldn't help but laugh. He seemed to feel perfectly content among her friends, but he also stood apart somehow.

Since the first day he'd walked into Club B, Benjamin had oozed an enigmatic presence that made her aware of him. Except now she wasn't only aware of him, but he was aware of everything she did as well, controlled it even. Suddenly, the strange stretching feeling in her ass felt warmer and seemed to move toward her pussy. It was wrong and so damn hot. She scanned the card table, suddenly more intrigued by what directions the next card might contain.

"Looks like all seven teams managed round one, so every team can pick up a card for round two."

"Go ahead and pick one," Benjamin told her with a smirk. He knew all too well that walking with that thing in her butt was making the plug rub inside of her. She held back her mumbled "sadist" until she'd turned away from him, but the strange stretching in her backside felt as if he was holding on to her leash the entire way to and back from the table. A sign of his possession, of her submission.

Why did the reminder of her vulnerability in his hand not make her worry? It should. She knew that. She hardly knew the man, and yet the more time she spent with him, the more relaxed she felt under his command.

Jeffrey's voice interrupted her before she could start down the rabbit hole of questioning herself once again, and she was oddly grateful. She wanted to enjoy this evening. Something about Benjamin made her want to live in the moment, just like that time at Club B's party. She could worry about what happened afterward later.

"Turn over your cards now."

Again, she flipped the card over and held it so they could both read it.

Leading the submissive by their leash, the dominant member of the team will pick out a toy and choose another dominant to secure it to their submissive.

Jessica turned to watch Benjamin's reaction, but his expression stayed blank. She couldn't help herself, so she asked, "Does it bother you?"

"To allow another dominant's hands on your body?"

When she nodded, he kept speaking. "I don't particularly like sharing what's mine, but it's part of a game and since I get to choose the toy and the dominant, I'm okay with it. What about you?"

She paused. She hadn't actually considered how she felt about the task herself, too curious to see how Benjamin would react. Despite all her emotional reservations, she'd scened with plenty of men, so she didn't mind being touched by different people. It felt strange to have Benjamin watch her, though.

She remembered that day in Club B when she'd seen him scene with someone else, and she had to wonder if he'd feel even the tiniest sliver of jealousy seeing someone else touch her, the way she'd felt jealous seeing him touch another submissive. Except, she wasn't truly his. Just like this was a game, they were just playing at being a couple for the night. Perhaps that's why he didn't mind going through with this round of the game.

"What was that thought?" his stern voice interrupted her.

"Ah, I'm okay with it, I guess."

His brows drew together. "I don't like dishonesty. You looked as if you found the idea distasteful. Explain to me what exactly your thoughts were."

She swallowed. This was too awkward. If she told him she wanted him to feel jealous at the thought of her being touched by someone else, if she honestly explained to him that she felt rejected because he didn't think of her as belonging to him, she'd sound terribly needy. More than she'd probably already looked after the way she'd ran to him and knelt at his feet when he'd first arrived at the party.

She briefly glanced up to see him staring at her. At least he didn't look annoyed, but he also didn't exactly look encouraging. If she lied now and he noticed, he might cut their evening short and however much she didn't want to seem needy, she also didn't want this night to end yet. Who knew when the next time would be that she'd feel so free to enjoy herself with a dom?

"Jessica?" he prompted.

"Well, I was thinking that you probably didn't mind having someone else touch me because I'm not actually your submissive. You're just scening with me tonight because you wanted to help me out, not because you actually wanted *me*." She emphasized the last word, not daring to look up at him. The feeling of the plug in her ass grew uncomfortable. An unwanted reminder of how much she'd exposed herself to him, how easily she'd get hurt if he rejected her now.

"That thought bothers you? That I offered to scene with you to help you overcome your fears of truly submitting to a new dom?"

Startled, she looked up at him once more. "No, no, I didn't mean that. I really appreciate that you offered to help me."

She was sure he couldn't even fathom how much. She'd felt so lost, trying to determine how to move forward with someone. And then he'd stepped in and told her what to do. It had lifted an enormous weight off of her and made her relax with a man for the first time in a long time.

"If that isn't what bothers you, then it's because you think I don't desire you? That I'm helping you for an entirely selfless reason?" He paused, smiling at her. "Jessica, I desire you very much. You are a beautiful, intelligent woman whom I wanted to get to know right from the start. Why do you think I went along with Mistress Vivienne's suggestion at the party? Do you really think I would've come down to the dungeon to play with you, if I hadn't wanted to do a scene with you already? No, Jessica, I desire you."

"Oh." It was the only thing she could say. Her mind was blank, taken up entirely by the warm feeling spreading inside of her. Sure, she'd been desired by men who wanted to scene with her, but none of them had looked at her with such intensity as Benjamin was doing. He wasn't holding back his thoughts and emotions from her, wasn't keeping her guessing. Unlike Collin, Benjamin made himself as vulnerable and available to her as he expected from her in return.

But he also hadn't corrected her other comment. He didn't mind having someone else touch her because she wasn't actually his submissive. The possessive gestures she'd cherished were merely part of the dom-sub dance, not signs of his true claim on her.

"Is there something else that was bothering you?" he asked, and this time she'd steeled herself against the question.

"No, thank you for telling me that."

He reached up and cupped her face in his hands. "You're welcome, little one." Then he leaned forward and pressed a gentle kiss on her lips.

"We need to hurry, I think." Everyone else seemed busy attaching or receiving various nipple clamps, butterfly vibrators, and butt plugs.

"Actually, I've changed my mind. What do you say we support the other teams for the third round? Perhaps Mistress Vivienne and Sebastian?"

Surprised, she stared at him. "You want to forfeit?"

"No, little one, I just don't feel in the mood to share you anymore." Then he reached around and tugged on her tail. "Come on now."

Instead of leading her over to Vivienne and Sebastian, though, he led her to his toy bag.

"What are we doing here?" She could feel a smile tugging on her lips and she knew she should probably be more worried about what other toys he had in that bag, but right now, she just felt too happy to be nervous.

"Just because I don't want someone else to attach the toy doesn't mean I don't want to see you wearing something else."

He pulled out a pair of nipple clamps with pretty black diamonds hanging off them.

He grabbed her left breast and rolled her nipple between his fingers until it jutted out, then he placed the tweezer tips onto it and started closing the screw until she sucked in air. He loosened it slightly and repeated the process on the other side.

"Very pretty," he murmured, and heat rushed from her breasts down into her belly.

The timer sounded and Jeffrey called for the next round. Ignoring the others, Benjamin stepped closer to her, reaching around and cupping her ass. He pulled her against him and lowered his head until he could press a searing kiss on her lips. Jessica felt herself sag against him, opening her lips to allow his tongue entry. He swept into her mouth, taking possession of her, while his hand kneaded her butt, jiggling the butt plug in a way that made her desire soar.

When he let go, she was a panting mess and his eyes were hooded and gleaming with desire.

"To hell with supporting another team." He took her hand and pulled her further back into the dungeon. A giggle escaped her as she allowed him to lead her to a spanking bench.

"Hop on."

Jessica felt almost giddy as she got onto the bench. Her legs spread, she knelt on the padded leg rests. Then she tipped her upper body forward to rest on the cushioned top that angled down slightly. She was careful not to put any weight on her clamped nipples. After all, there was no need to torture herself when she had a dom all to herself for the rest of the night who was clearly looking forward to doing it himself.

Her position left her ass high in the air, and she could feel the tail hanging down between her legs. Benjamin made a humming noise of approval and Jessica turned her head down, hiding her smile. He moved around the bench, fastening the restraints, then stepped behind her.

Running his hands down her back, his fingers reminded her of the way the Wartenberg wheel had felt earlier. Somehow her arousal grew even more intense, and she knew Benjamin would be able to spot the wetness if he looked beneath the fluffy tail attached to her ass, but he just kept stroking her until she could feel every last one of her muscles relax.

When he stepped back, Jessica couldn't bring herself to worry about what he'd planned for her. She was much too comfortable, despite the restraints and clamps. All she wanted was to feel his hands back on her.

And then she did.

His hand slapped against her upper left thigh and the startling sting made her want to jump up. Held in place by the restraints, she could do nothing but wait for the second slap. When it came, she tried to relax her muscles to lessen the sting. Feeling her compliance, Benjamin murmured words of praise and she settled into the spanking. He avoided the plug in her butt, but she could still feel the toy move each time her butt cheeks jiggled from the impact of his hand.

She rolled her forehead against the leather of the bench and lost herself in the rhythmic sensation.

Just when she was about to drift off to space, lost in the feeling of pain and pleasure, Benjamin stopped and instead tugged on the butt plug. She moaned, unsure if in pleasure or distress. When he kept wiggling the plug, slowly inching it out and then sliding it back in, the heat in her core coiled, ready to release.

His second hand pressed between her legs, finding her most intimate spot, and started circling the sensitive nub. Moaning, she tried to press back, to increase the sensation, but she couldn't move, just feel. It was the best type of torture there was.

"Now, tell me Jessica. I've told you that I desire you, that I want you. Do you want me? Do you desire me?"

"Oh god, yes, yes, I do." It was an easy question. She wanted to feel him inside of her, wanted him to fill her, to make her come on his cock.

Again, she strained backwards, and again, she couldn't move. It made her clench her pussy and Benjamin let go of the butt plug to give her a light slap against her wet lower lips. Her yell was one of pleasure and surprise, and she was so much closer to the precipice than before.

"Good. I like that answer, little one." With that, he pulled out the butt plug in one swift motion and, almost simultaneously, plunged himself into her pussy. She screamed as the first wave of her orgasm hit her. Without pausing, Benjamin took her with long, hard strokes, riding out her orgasm until he joined her.

When she came by a little while later, Jessica knew one thing for certain. She desired Benjamin, all of him, not just his body. She wasn't sure she was ready for the intensity of that feeling, but she wasn't willing to fight it just then. Instead, she just snuggled into his powerful arms and the soft blanket he'd wrapped around her, drifting high on the feeling of being with her Master.

CHAPTER TWELVE

A fter spending the rest of the night at Jeffrey's, chatting with everyone and looking at the new furniture
pieces Jeffrey had designed, Jessica was exhausted.

She was curled into a blanket on Jeffrey's couch, leaning her head against Benjamin's shoulder, while he discussed his dungeon plans with Jeffrey and Vivienne. Jeffrey's sub for the night had already left and Sebastian was
chatting with some other submissives, but Jessica felt too
spent to get up.

Tonight had been amazing, but now that she was sitting
here, she knew one thing with perfect clarity. While she'd
wanted to take Benjamin up on his offer to help her get
over her hang-up of trusting men, she'd done the one
thing she'd been afraid of. She was falling in love with him
already. Instead of slowly easing into trusting him, she'd
plunged right into the deep end. Somewhere deep inside
her she knew she wanted to submit to him, to please him,
to be his.

How was she supposed to keep a calm head going into
a relationship, when her heart and body were screaming
they wanted to go all in? And what if he wasn't interested
in her the same way? Desiring was one thing, but she'd
gone and fallen for him. She could hardly expect him to

feel the same way. It was insanity after they'd only known each other for such a short time.

As she listened to him discuss his home, feeling the vibration of his voice under her cheek, she realized that she'd never even been to his house. The only places she'd seen Benjamin were her club, the restaurant, and here. Each time, other people had surrounded them, except for the brief car ride to the restaurant.

They'd never gone on an actual date, nor had he invited her into his life. They'd been to *her* club, *her* favorite restaurant, and now they were at *her* friend's home. She'd invited Benjamin into her life, but he hadn't done the same for her. And why would he? He hadn't asked to date her or for her to be his submissive. He'd generously offered her his help and had wanted to scene with her. She couldn't expect him to fall for her as recklessly and fast as she had done for him.

She wrapped her arms around herself and lifted her head. Immediately, Benjamin stopped whatever he'd been saying and turned to her with a smile. "Are you all right? Thirsty?"

"Uh, no, I'm not thirsty, thank you. It's getting late, so I think I'll drive home now."

Benjamin scrutinized her expression for a moment, and she worked hard to keep her expression from showing her racing thoughts. Eventually, he nodded.

"It's been a long evening. I'll walk you to your car and head home myself."

Turning to Jeffrey and Vivienne, he inclined his head. "Jeffrey, thank you very much for inviting me tonight. It was a very enjoyable evening." He squeezed her leg as he said it, and Jessica tried hard not to blush.

"I'll get an order from you, I suspect?" Jeffrey said, grinning.

Benjamin laughed. "You will indeed. I'll send you an email tomorrow."

Vivienne rose. "May I?" she asked Benjamin, and Jessica wanted to interrupt and tell her she wasn't Benjamin's submissive. The evening was over now, so she didn't need to get his permission to hug her best friend goodbye, but Benjamin nodded, and for some reason his response caused a twinge of pain in her heart.

This feeling was the worst irony of it all. Her ex fiancé had tried to control everything about her life and she'd kicked him to the curb, and now here she was desperately wanting Benjamin to keep doing it for a little while longer. She wasn't a newbie to the lifestyle, and she knew that there was nothing wrong with being a submissive woman if there was consent in the relationship, but it looked like her past baggage had messed with her more than she'd ever realized.

Vivienne's arms wrapped around her and she whispered in her ear. "I'll come by your place tomorrow morning and we'll talk."

It wasn't a question, and Jessica loved her best friend even more for it. Yes, she'd need to have a good long girls chat about this. Maybe Vivienne could help her figure out what she should do next.

When Vivienne let her go, Benjamin took her arm and led her to the front door. Jeffrey handed them both their coats, and they stepped onto the street, bringing their evening together to an end.

"My car is down that way," Jessica said, pointing to where she'd parked her vehicle half-way down the street.

"All right, let's go."

She felt his eyes on her as they walked, but couldn't think of what to say.

"You're rather quiet, Jessica. I thought we had a very nice evening. Am I missing something or are your doubts about opening up returning?"

It was a good question.

Were these the same doubts she'd had before, or were they different? Before, she'd worried that she'd never again be able to bring herself to trust another dom enough to be truly happy. And now? She no longer needed to question whether she could open herself up to a new dom emotionally, because she knew that if Benjamin asked her to, she wouldn't hold anything back from him.

Each time he took control, she felt lighter, more herself. She wanted him with every fibre of her body, because she trusted him. Benjamin was a good, ethical dom, but she realized now that she hadn't been naïve about who Collin was in the beginning, either. She'd known and trusted her ex, and it still hadn't been enough. Collin had portrayed himself to have those same characteristics she liked about Benjamin, and only time had shown her that he wasn't true to the persona he'd played. It hadn't been her fault. She'd been misled, but it still stung.

There was a difference, though. While Collin had wanted to dominate her and take over her decisions, Benjamin wanted to help her instead. With him, giving up control was gaining control over her life, because instead of taking away her choices, he added to them by freeing up her mental space for more. Back when she'd started seeing Collin, it had felt good to give up some of the burden of being responsible for everything in her life, but he'd taken more and more freedoms away from her until she'd felt like she was suffocating.

Benjamin was like a breeze of fresh air. She just wasn't sure if he might blow right past her.

What she needed to figure out was whether she was brave enough to see if he was interested in more than helping her overcome her hang-ups and scene occasionally. Whether she was courageous enough to risk falling even deeper in love with a man who might move on once she wasn't in need of his help anymore. She couldn't make that decision right now, while she was still basking in the afterglow of her orgasm. She needed to have a good night's sleep and perhaps talk with Vivienne to help her keep a clear head.

"I enjoyed our evening, thank you. I'm just tired, that's all. I'll see you at the club on Wednesday, though, right?" she asked, even though a voice in her yelled that Wednesday was much too long a wait. She knew she couldn't force herself on him and if she'd only see him on Wednesday, she'd at least have enough time to consider what she wanted to do.

"Actually, I would like you to join me at my house tomorrow. I believe we should have a conversation about us. I understand you have been out of the dating game for a while, but I think we're well matched and I like you Jessica. I'd like to discuss if you think there is the potential for us to explore things further."

Jessica felt herself freeze in place. "You mean you'd like for us to date?" It was the exact question she hadn't been sure she'd be brave enough to ask, but now he'd just about answered it for her already.

His smile grew. "Yes, little one. I'd be interested if you are."

She wanted to jump into his arms and yell yes, but she held back. She didn't know what dating would look like with Benjamin. He was a dominant, a Master, and that meant he'd want control and she didn't know how much. She also didn't know how much she was willing to

135

give up, even if she knew that she ultimately craved his control. She might trust him, but could she trust herself to make a wise decision for herself?

She gave him a shaky smile. Maybe it was coming down from all those endorphins that her body had released during the scene, but right now, she felt slightly unstable.

"Sure, I'd like to talk tomorrow. If you text me your address and a time, I'll meet you at your place." She could give him, and herself, that much. A chance to talk about it, a chance for her heart to get what it wanted. More time with Benjamin.

After another moment of him scrutinizing her, he nodded. "Are you safe to drive?"

She paused a moment to check herself. She was feeling exhausted and her emotions were all over the place, but she'd be okay. "I am."

As she drove past him, she lifted her hand and waved. It felt like a strange ending to an evening that had involved such intimacy between them.

Benjamin unlocked his front door and dropped his toy bag inside his entrance area. The evening had gone very well until Jessica had said she needed to go home. She hadn't retreated like that first time they'd played, but something in her eyes had told him she'd needed some distance, and that was exactly what he didn't want to see, because the more she submitted to him, the more he wanted her.

And she'd submitted beautifully tonight. The way she'd fallen to her knees for him when he'd arrived had been one of the most humbling experiences he'd ever had with a sub.

The question was how he should proceed. He couldn't pressure her to feel the same way as he did, because what he wanted more than anything was true loyalty and that had to be gifted, not taken. If he came on too strong, she might back up, but she also needed him to be dominant and lead her toward happiness. Because if she decided to give a relationship with him a shot, he was sure they could both be happy. They were a great match, and he'd do everything in his power to make sure she'd see that.

He took off his jacket and headed to his bedroom. He really needed a shower. Undressing, he took in the empty nightstands and dresser. Back in L.A. he had his home filled with family pictures, but since his move he hadn't wanted to put up those photos, the memories of the way his sister and father had confronted him were too bitter.

The only photo in his home now was that of his mother in the living room. She'd passed when he was a teenager, but he still missed her. It was probably good she hadn't been around for what had happened with Victoria. Or, maybe, things would have been different if she had been.

In some ways, today had been a similar evening to the day his family had turned on him. He and Victoria had attended a play party. They'd been seeing each other for a few months and Benjamin had thought they were about ready to take the next step. He'd actually been prepared to discuss a more permanent arrangement with her and had been sure she'd agree. She already knew his family since she worked for his father, and it had seemed like a perfect fit.

When she'd first come to Master Hell's dungeon, he'd been surprised to see her familiar face. He'd met her at some of his father's company functions, not knowing she was into the lifestyle. After spotting him, she'd come over to say hello, and they'd hit it off. They'd quickly started dating and had been going to play parties whenever they had a chance.

That night, Victoria had come home with him to continue the evening. In the car, she'd intentionally been a smart ass, angling for a funishment, and Benjamin had been looking forward to giving her what she wanted. When they'd arrived, he'd stepped into his place and ordered her to strip, not surprised by the lights being already turned on. He forgot to turn them off often enough that it hadn't seemed weird.

Victoria had fallen to her knees in a perfect show of surrender. He still remembered her giggling question. "Will I be getting my spanking now, Master?"

"You deserve my hand on your ass, you little brat," he'd said, just as his sister's shocked, "What the hell?" had sounded from behind them.

When he'd turned around, he'd seen Bernadette and his father coming out of the kitchen. Later, he'd learned that his aunt had had a minor car accident that night and had been admitted to the nearby hospital. His sister had decided that they should stay at Benjamin's house for the night to be nearby and pick their aunt up first thing in the morning. His father had a key to his place, so they'd let themselves in after Benjamin hadn't answered the door.

The stone-faced expression on his father's face had been enough to send Victoria scrambling out of the door without even a word of goodbye. When Bernadette had repeated her question, "What the hell, Ben?", he'd explained calmly that Victoria and he had a consensual relationship involving BDSM. He'd always had a close relationship with his family, so he hadn't felt the need to make up a lie now that they'd seen him with Victoria.

"You mean you're into BDSM? Like whipping women and shit?" his sister had exclaimed, obviously horrified. His father had sat there, his expression still frozen.

"Nothing I do with women isn't something they haven't clearly consented to," he'd defended himself, and an awkward silence had stretched out between them.

Then his father had gotten up, not having said a word, and had nodded to Bernadette, "Let's go home."

Benjamin had figured he should give them a night to digest what he'd shared with them, but when no one had answered the phone the next day, he'd driven to his father's house.

"You're not welcome to come in. I raised you better than to want to hit women. You need to get help," his father had said after answering the door.

It had been a huge punch to the gut. His family was supposed to know him better than anyone else, and yet they'd suddenly looked at him as if he was a bad person. As if the consensual kink he engaged in turned him into some sort of awful predator who took advantage of vulnerable women.

When he'd gotten back home, he'd called Victoria. If they went to his father's house together, it might be easier to explain. If his father heard it from her, he'd understand. After all, he knew her. She'd worked for his father for years, and he respected her for her intelligence and work ethic. His father had even been hopeful their relationship would get more serious.

But when he'd called, Victoria had only told him that she'd sent her resignation to his father that morning and that she wouldn't return to Master Hell's dungeon either.

She'd not only left him, but she'd left him hanging when he'd needed her support the most.

He'd moved to Toronto a couple months later.

Wanting to wash away the memories of Victoria and his family, Benjamin turned the water in his shower to hot, but now that he'd opened the door to memory lane, he couldn't help but compare his feelings toward Jessica to the situation with Victoria. When Victoria had left him, he'd learned how much disloyalty hurt, but he'd also realized that he couldn't tolerate someone who didn't have the spine to stand up for their partner.

Sure, he understood that there were good reasons for people to be in the BDSM closet, and that was perfectly fine, but when someone you supposedly loved needed you the most, then you needed to be there for them. Jessica was that kind of person. She stood up for her club members and she was proud of her role in their community. Benjamin couldn't picture her backing away if someone needed her.

Only could he convince her that she needed him? That he would be there for her and share in some of the responsibilities that were weighing her down?

When he got out of the shower and dried himself off, he went back into his bedroom, where his cell lay on the dresser. He picked it up and typed a text message.

Be at my place at 1pm tomorrow. I'll have lunch for you. Thank you for the lovely evening.

He added his address and put his phone down. She'd already agreed to come. Now he just needed to figure out what he'd say tomorrow to make her want to stay.

CHAPTER THIRTEEN

The next morning, Jessica opened the door for Vivienne, who was carrying a cardboard holder with two cups of coffee and a bag with, what Jessica hoped, were pastries.

"Morning," Vivienne said cheerfully. "Your office or upstairs?"

"Let's sit in my office." Jessica loved the seating area in her office and often used it as if it were her living room when she had guests.

Vivienne led the way, putting her breakfast offerings on the coffee table while Jessica went to grab a couple of plates and then joined her friend. When they each held a steaming cup of coffee and had a pastry in front of them, Vivienne gave Jessica an expectant look. "Spill, girlfriend."

"I like him."

The three words came out sounding like a sigh, but Vivienne's mouth turned into a wide smile. "That's great. So why don't you look happy? I thought this was what you wanted? To find a dom for yourself."

"It was. I mean, it is. And he wants to see where this is going, too. I'm going to his place for lunch to discuss things." She put her hands up to place quotation marks around the words 'discuss things'.

"Okay, so then again my question. Why don't you look happy? It seems like everything is going well for you. You certainly looked pretty content last night!" Vivienne waggled her brows.

A grin forced itself onto Jessica's lips. All morning she'd had flashbacks to last night. "He's damn good."

"So what are you worried about?"

Jessica shrugged. "I guess I don't even know myself. It all seems to be so easy. I guess I'm waiting for the other shoe to drop. What if he wants more control than I'm willing to give up? Or if I'm needier than he's ready for?"

Now it was Vivienne's turn to shrug. "That's what conversations are for. You discuss your limits and expectations and then determine if you're a good fit. Your kinks seem to line up nicely so far, there is no reason to think you won't find a good middle ground for the rest."

"I suppose you're right," Jessica agreed, but she couldn't quite make herself look into Vivienne's eyes.

"Jessica," her friend's voice snapped, and Jessica's eyes flew up automatically. "Girlfriend, you are freaking yourself out and it's not doing you any favors. If you don't think you're ready to express your expectations with Master Benjamin, then let's talk about them now, so you have a better idea what you want to say to him later."

Relief washed over her. Technically, each time she'd talked to Benjamin it had been incredibly easy, so she didn't know why this should be different, except that she knew more than her head would be involved in the conversation, and last time she'd been in love it had ended in a huge disaster. Talking with Vivienne would make sure at least one person would evaluate what she was saying with a calm mind.

"Okay, thank you." Now she met Vivienne's smile with one of her own.

"Do you want the power dynamic to be limited strictly to the bedroom?" her friend prompted.

Jessica shook her head. "No, I've always wanted someone who'd stay in the dynamic outside the bedroom too, but not a slave dynamic or a full on service sub kind of thing. Just sexual submission and someone who takes over when things get stressful, you know?"

Vivienne nodded. "You know enough about my relationship with Sebastian. Is that the type of dynamic you want?"

She'd often spent time with Vivienne and her sub Sebastian and longed to have what they had, but it'd never been exactly what she'd been missing. "Well, almost, just, I guess I wouldn't mind something a bit more structured. I know you're Sebastian's domme all the time, but you're keeping things really flexible. I think I'd feel better with more precise guidelines as to what he would expect of me."

"It sounds like you already know what you want," Vivienne said, her expression thoughtful. "So why not just tell Master Benjamin and go from there?"

"Because when my ex did it, I hated it. So what if I just think I want those things and it'll actually feel suffocating?" The words burst out of her as if a dam had broken that had tried to keep her insecurity hidden from her friend.

She wanted to give up control, and logically she knew it was okay to feel that way, but her subconscious was warning her off, because when Collin had been trying to assert his control, it had stifled her entire life. In hindsight, she knew her ex hadn't been acting like a sanc dom, but at the time, the boundaries of what she'd felt comfortable with and what he'd done had felt a whole lot less clear.

"Jessica, you're a smart woman who runs a successful business. If you need to renegotiate the terms of your relationship later on, then you can do that. Do you not trust Master Benjamin to listen to you if you need to discuss things with him?"

"I think I can trust him. I mean, I have no reason not to. He's been nothing but kind and straight-forward with me, but I haven't known him for very long. What if I'm rushing into this relationship because I'm falling in love with him?"

Vivienne's eyes widened. "You love him? Jess, that's wonderful." Vivienne got up from her spot and came to sit right next to her, taking her hand. "Look, there is nothing wrong with taking your time to get to know him, and you can do that on your own terms. There is no right or wrong way to do this. If you want to explore a relationship with him that involves stricter BDSM rules, than that is fine. You'll just have to take it one step at a time and make sure he earns your trust first. You won't be alone either. I'm here to watch out for you and so are Jeffrey, Sebastian, and the others."

The words were soothing Jessica's worries and she turned to smile at her friend, but Vivienne wasn't done yet. "You're right to be careful. Unfortunately, there are people in this lifestyle who can't be trusted, but there are also a lot of amazing doms out there, and I think Master Benjamin is one of them. Tell him what you want and listen to what he wants, in turn. Then you can decide together how you want to build up to that type of relationship. And know that if you ever feel like you're in too deep, you can talk to him. If he doesn't listen, talk to your friends and we will make sure he hears what you have to say."

Jessica blinked away the tears welling in her eyes. "I don't think he's the type of man who wouldn't listen."

Vivienne smiled again. "I know, otherwise I wouldn't tell you to give him a shot."

When Jessica parked her car in front of Benjamin's house, she felt none of the heaviness that had weighed her down at the end of last night. Her chat with Vivienne had left her hopeful.

Benjamin had all but said he wanted to take her on as his submissive, and what was more, he actually wanted them to date. Now she just needed to figure out the details, and after she'd already practiced that part with Vivienne, she didn't see why this shouldn't work out too.

She took a deep breath and rang the doorbell. Almost immediately she heard footsteps and her stomach did a weird lurch.

"Jessica, hello. Come on in. I hope you had a pleasant drive?"

"Hi, I did, thanks." She handed off her coat and looked around the spacious room. It was an open concept kitchen and living room, with a small entrance area for coats and shoes. She could see the dining table already set with plates and glasses, and a delicious smell wafted over from the stove.

Benjamin noticed her looking and grinned. "I'm making rosemary chicken. I figured chicken is a fairly safe bet."

"You're right. It smells delicious. I'm impressed. I'm not much of a cook myself, unfortunately."

"I'd enjoy teaching you."

She smiled at him and Benjamin led her into the room and over to the dining table. "Take a seat. The food is almost ready to be served. Can I get you something to drink first? I have wine, sparkling water, and juice."

"A sparkling water would be lovely, thanks."

Benjamin busied himself pouring them both drinks and then plating the food. She watched him move around the kitchen. He was as self assured here as he was in the club and it was hard not to notice the play of his muscles under his tight shirt. He was wearing jeans and socks, the casual domestic look making her mouth water for something other than rosemary chicken.

When he put a plate in front of her, she hardly glanced down, too focused on him to think about the food. He gave her a knowing grin, and she felt the telltale heat of a blush. It was really quite ridiculous how easily she got flustered.

"Enjoy," Benjamin said, gesturing to her plate, forcing her to actually look down.

"Oh, this looks amazing, and it smells divine. Thank you for cooking for me."

"It's my pleasure. Now eat, before it gets cold."

She took a bite of the chicken and rice before eating some of the buttered carrots. It was as good as it smelled, and she told him as much. After that, Benjamin did some small talk, but she couldn't concentrate, too anxious for the conversation to come. Eventually, Benjamin let out a huff.

"Jessica, would you feel better if we discussed our relationship? You look like you'd rather chew your fingernails than eat the lunch I made."

Embarrassed, she looked up. "The food is amazing. It really is. I guess I'm just a bit nervous."

"Let's go and sit on the couch then. I'll clean this up later."

She considered protesting and offering her help with cleaning, but decided she really did want to have this conversation first. If she didn't, she'd lose all the confidence she'd won from her conversation with Vivienne.

When he led her over to the sectional, she settled onto the couch, while Benjamin took the armchair that stood at a ninety-degree angle. He was close, but still giving her some space, and she appreciated it. It would help her keep her focus on their conversation.

"Little one, if the thought of discussing a potential relationship with me makes you this anxious, I need you to be honest with me, because I want to make myself clear. I am interested in you, but I have no intention of placing any pressure on you. I know you've got stuff you need to work through, and if you want, I'm happy to help with that, but what I don't want is someone who isn't sure they want to be with me. I've had that in the past and it didn't work out well."

His face was calm, but she could see a moment of sadness flash in his eyes, and there was no missing the seriousness in his tone. "If you agree to be with me, we will discuss limits, but I expect total loyalty and nothing less. I'm a dominant, and I have no intention of pretending to be anyone else. If you consent to be with me, I expect your obedience and submission in exchange for my care. All within the boundaries of what we agree on, of course. If you aren't sure you can commit to a relationship like that and really devote yourself to it, you should let me know now."

He paused for a moment to study her, and she knew she probably looked slightly panicked. He wanted absolute loyalty, and she wanted to promise him that, because her heart told her he was a man who deserved such devotion, but how could she do that if her brain couldn't be one hundred percent sure he wouldn't eventually place demands on her that she wasn't willing to accept.

She remembered Collin's outraged words when she'd called off their engagement. *You're mine, you said you wanted to be mine. You agreed. I've done nothing more than look after you. It's what you wanted. And now you're stabbing me in the back as if you didn't ask for it. Wanted it.*

The theory of open communication and consent was one thing. She'd told countless club members how important it was to keep those communication channels open throughout a relationship, but it felt different now that Benjamin wanted her assurance. Something she thought she wanted today might feel different tomorrow, so to promise him absolute commitment to their agreements felt wrong.

Her pause was obviously long enough to give away her doubts. Disappointment flashed across Benjamin's face, but he quickly schooled his features. "Don't worry, little one. It's okay if you want to move slow or rather be friends."

Except she didn't. Wasn't that what Vivienne had said? They should discuss their expectations and then figure out steps to get there? They could take things slow and she could allow him a chance to earn her trust. She pushed her chin up and forced herself to look him in his eyes.

"I want to see where this is going, but taking things slow would be a good start," she said, happy to see his face change into a pleased smile. "I'm just nervous because I haven't actually dated someone in a rather long time and I really enjoy being with you. But I think I still need to figure out where my limits are when it comes to a relationship that goes beyond the club, you know?"

Benjamin nodded, then moved off the armchair to sit next to her, taking hold of her hand and intertwining their fingers. "That sounds good to me. Now tell me what you'd eventually like to have in terms of a D/s dynamic, even if that isn't something you are quite ready for yet."

Jessica watched their hands that were now resting on his leg. His skin was warm and his huge hand made her small one almost disappear. She liked the strength that he seemed to emanate, and she decided that she might as well take advantage of his nearness. She leaned a little toward him until their shoulders touched and she felt more of his heat warming her. When she looked up at him, she saw the approval in his eyes.

"I've always wanted a D/s dynamic that goes beyond the bedroom. I like our sexual dynamic very much, and eventually I'm sure I'd like to try out more things together, like impact play and bondage, maybe even some suspension," she remembered how he'd told her he was looking to add suspension hooks to his dungeon room and briefly wondered if he'd show her that room today, before she continued, "but when it comes to the other stuff, outside of the dungeon or bedroom, I think I'd like something in the middle between vanilla and slave. Not a service sub, but to have rules around the house that would take the thinking out of things if that makes sense."

"I understand, and I'm happy to hear it. I think what you're describing would work well for me too, but I don't mind taking things slow until we get there. I know this is new, but it helps to have these types of conversations early on. We can always adjust as we go and figure out how much control would work well for our dynamic for a more 24/7 situation. The main thing is not to jump in head first, but to commit to give this a proper shot. I'm not interested in a fling, Jessica. I want a submissive who's willing to commit to me long-term."

Jessica was about to ask what Benjamin thought taking things slow might look like for them when his doorbell rang. Benjamin looked at the door with a surprised expression.

"I'm not expecting anyone, and on a Sunday, there shouldn't be any deliveries. Give me a second." With that, he rose and walked toward the entrance area.

Jessica twisted so she could see the door, too. When Benjamin opened it, she saw a pretty, athletic woman standing outside. The woman was wearing yoga pants and boots under her parka, and she was holding the handle of a small carry-on suitcase. Jessica's stomach gave a lurch and she could feel herself tense. If the woman had a suitcase, she obviously expected to be staying here. With Benjamin.

Quickly, Jessica looked to see Benjamin's expression. He looked shocked, maybe angry, but also a little hopeful, perhaps.

Was this woman an ex of his? Would he ask her in, even though Jessica was sitting in his living room and they'd just discussed getting together? She supposed he'd never once mentioned that he wanted a monogamous relationship, and she hadn't made that clear either.

How stupid was she? Many people in the lifestyle had more than one partner. She should have clarified that that was a hard limit for her, but she hadn't even thought of it. She'd looked at Benjamin and hadn't even pictured the possibility of him being with another woman.

Until now.

CHAPTER FOURTEEN

"**B**ernadette, what are you doing here?"

"We need to talk, Ben." The brunette hadn't noticed Jessica yet, but as she spoke, Benjamin looked over to the couch, and the woman's head swiveled to take Jessica in.

"Now isn't a good time." His voice was flat in a way Jessica had never heard it. Sure he measured his voice usually, but now he sounded as if he was drained of all emotion, and it felt like she was the one intruding on something, rather than being Benjamin's guest who had every right to sit here on his couch. Or his submissive, who had a right to know why another woman was coming to his door with a suitcase in hand, needing to speak to him.

"I see." The woman's expression grew stony. "Is she your slave, then?"

Even though the brunette had lowered her voice, Jessica understood the words just fine and blanched as their meaning hit her. Slave, not submissive. Still, she couldn't tear her eyes off the scene in front of her. It looked as if the other woman was trying to hold back her emotions, but the derision in her expression was still apparent.

It wasn't often that someone you didn't know made that kind of assumption about you, and it added fire to the burning discomfort Jessica felt at witnessing the confrontation. The woman clearly knew Benjamin was a dominant, perhaps even knew more about his interests than Jessica did. Chances were the other woman was well-acquainted with him, though the discomfort at the suggestion of someone being in a Master slave relationship Jessica had seen in her face suggested that she wasn't part of their lifestyle.

"That's enough, Bernadette. I don't know why you think you can just show up here, but I won't discuss anything with you right now, especially if you only came here to confront me about the lifestyle I chose. Or insult my guests, for that matter."

After a second, the woman's features smoothed out. "I didn't come to fight with you, Ben. It's a mess at home and I needed to come here and speak with you. I want to try to understand why you left us for this." She gestured toward Jessica.

It felt like the brunette was throwing punches at her, and Jessica had no idea how she'd even ended up in the fight, except that it sounded a whole lot as if this woman and Benjamin had shared a life with each other. And that Benjamin had apparently been in a Master slave relationship before.

"Perhaps I should leave," Jessica murmured as she got up from her spot on the couch. She wasn't sure how to get past them, but this was obviously not a good time to talk about a new relationship for Benjamin, and she had no intention of getting in the way of whatever this was.

"No, sit down," Benjamin snapped and her legs almost buckled under the stare he shot in her direction.

"Let the woman leave if she wants to," the brunette all but yelled. "You cannot hold her against her will, too."

Jessica fought the urge to sit down, unsure whether she should obey him. Despite their scenes, they weren't in a D/s relationship yet, and even though she wanted to be with him, right now alarm bells were ringing in her head.

When Benjamin spoke, his voice was icy. "What do you mean *too*?" It was the same question that had been rattling in Jessica's brain.

"What you did with Victoria wasn't right. She told dad when she resigned, you know. That she didn't want to do this anymore. You can't force women into being your slaves if they don't agree to it. I've read up on it, on consent in BDSM. And if you trick women into this, it's not right. If this woman wants to leave, she's allowed to leave."

Jessica could feel her breathing growing ragged, the tension she'd felt since the woman had arrived mounting to outright distress. Memories of the way she'd run into this situation before flashed in her mind. How she'd looked for a dom, a man who'd seemed perfect but who'd started to treat her more and more like his personal property as time went by. Like a slave. It hadn't been what she'd wanted.

She needed to leave and have room to think.

When she stepped up to the door and reached for her coat, Benjamin's hand closed around her arm. "Jessica," he warned.

"Are you serious?" the brunette fumed. "I came here to talk to you. To understand you. But this? This isn't right, Ben. You can't keep doing this to women."

Jessica shook off his arm and shot him an apologetic look. She didn't want to think the worst of him, but right now, she needed him to deal with this woman while she calmed herself down. She wanted some time to rationally think about his offer and the things she'd just heard. It looked like Jessica's presence was only riling the brunette up and that couldn't be helpful if he wanted to smooth things over with that woman. Or get rid of her, whichever. It was best if she gave them some room.

"I'm sorry. I think it's best I go now and let you figure things out between the two of you."

His expression grew cold, and she took a step back. "I'm asking you to stay. If you go now, we're done."

The ultimatum made icy hands claw at her insides. He was trying to intimidate and manipulate her consent, and she'd promised herself never to tolerate that again. She walked past the woman to her car.

Benjamin didn't call her back.

Benjamin was trying hard not to punch something. This weekend had gone to hell within the blink of an eye, or rather the ringing of his doorbell.

He still couldn't believe Jessica had just walked out. It'd been exactly like what Victoria had done when confronted with his family's prejudice. And now his sister was in his house, wanting to talk to him, as if she hadn't already said enough today.

He'd been intent on sending her on her way after Jessica had left. The prospect of exchanging one more word with her had been enough to send his blood pressure through the roof, but Bernadette had pushed her way in, saying she needed to use the bathroom. Now he stood in his own living room, trying to figure out what the hell to do about this whole mess.

He heard the faucet turn off in the bathroom and his sister emerged, looking less confrontational, even wearing a small, slightly awkward smile.

"Look, Ben, I didn't come here to fight. Honestly. I didn't tell you that I booked a flight, because I thought you might not want to see me."

"So you're not only presuming to know what I'm thinking, you've also chosen to ignore it." He gave her a stare that made women in the clubs he went to fall to their knees. Not his sister though, she just shrugged.

"I love you and I hate that you just moved away."

"I didn't just move away for no reason, and it's a bit hard to believe that you love me if you're also convinced I'm an abuser."

She had the decency to look uncomfortable. "I may have been hasty in judging you."

"You think? And what was that just now?" He swung out his arm to point to the door where Jessica had walked out of his life.

"I didn't think you'd already found another woman who'd be with you," Bernadette murmured, and a flash of pain hit him.

His own family considered him so vile in his interests that they didn't think he'd find a woman to want to be with him. And it looked like they weren't even wrong. He'd thought that Jessica, who proudly owned a BDSM club, would certainly stick up for him, but instead she'd left just as quickly as Victoria had.

Apparently, he wasn't the type of man anyone believed in.

Without another word, he turned to his kitchen. Opening the fridge, he grabbed two beers, holding one out for his sister. "Here."

He felt tired all of a sudden, no longer in the mood for a confrontation.

"Thank you." Bernadette walked to the couch and sat down where Jessica had sat less than fifteen minutes before. What a mess.

He had no energy left for fighting his sister's prejudices right now. He wouldn't apologize for his interests, but it felt damn hard to defend the special connection he'd always thought he could have with a sub, when each woman he chose for himself walked away from him so easily. When Jessica had walked out after they'd just talked about a future together.

A D/s relationship had to be grounded in trust, and he obviously couldn't trust any of the women he'd wanted to be with to actually support him in turn.

"Why are you here, Bernadette? You say you researched BDSM, but apparently you still think I'm doing something wrong, so what do you want from me?"

His sister looked down at her hands, shifting uncomfortably. "I already told you. I wanted to let you explain."

Benjamin snorted. "Oh yeah? Or did you want me to defend myself? Because so far, it's sounded a lot more like you're attacking me."

Now she looked up, obviously frustrated. "Look, I get it, okay? I'm not exactly easy on you, but it's not like I knew anything about this before Victoria, and when I started googling this stuff, it all sounded a lot more intense than what I expected, so I guess I'm kind of freaked out."

Taking a long gulp from his beer, he contemplated his answer. He'd moved away from L.A. after his father had made it clear he was no longer welcome in his childhood home. At the time, he hadn't understood why neither his father nor his sister had allowed him to explain what a D/s dynamic looked like. Now his sister was here. Still prejudiced, but she was here.

He sighed. At least this couldn't get any worse.

"What you said earlier, about consent. You're right about that. Except when the couple is into BDSM, consent isn't always expressed in the same way as in a vanilla relationship. If a submissive woman truly wants me to stop being in command, she'll use her safe word. Usually that's red, but it can be anything, really."

"But why?" his sister asked, leaning forward. She was listening, and Benjamin supposed it was the most he could expect.

"Because that way a submissive who enjoys intense stuff can say things like 'no' and 'don't', knowing it won't actually stop what we're doing." He took a gulp of his beer. Discussing BDSM with his sister was about as comfortable as grating his nuts with a cheese grinder, even if he appreciated that she was finally willing to listen. "Look, I'm not going into detail, but some things in BDSM can get intense, and sometimes part of it involves pretending one wants to stop. It's important that communication doesn't get misinterpreted, so we agree on a safe word beforehand."

For a moment Bernadette just sat there, looking at the wall across from her. "I've never thought you're a bad person, and for the record, after we saw you and Victoria together I was going to talk to you the next day, but then dad got that email from her."

Now Bernadette gave him a concerned look. "She quit her job and said she couldn't live with this shame anymore. It sounded like all the stuff dad taught us about how abused women blame themselves and are ashamed of being victims. I mean, she moved away from L.A. You have to admit, it looked like she was trying to get away from you. You know Dad freaked out, and I guess I just didn't know what to believe anymore. And then I saw all that slave stuff. How could anyone want to be treated like that?"

Draining the rest of the beer, Benjamin got up and walked to the window, staring out onto the parked cars outside. How could he make his sister see that BDSM wasn't demeaning, when she obviously couldn't emphasize with what the lifestyle was about?

"You're getting caught up in how different it is from the mainstream, instead of realizing that people get into BDSM because they find it offers them something that vanilla relationships don't give them. Some people enjoy pain, others find that when mixed with pleasure, pain can enhance a sexual experience for them. Do you really want to judge people for doing things that feel good to them?"

He couldn't believe he was having this conversation with his sister, but now that she'd made him talk, he needed her to understand. "A lot of BDSM is about the head space. I know it's hard to understand for many people, but submitting isn't about giving up control to someone else completely. A submissive, and even a slave, always has the option to withdraw their consent, and that with no fear of repercussions, otherwise it's abuse. Submissives choose to relinquish control because it allows them to experience sex and sometimes life more fully. By stepping away from the pressure of having to make all the decisions, they feel better." He trailed off, not turning around.

When Bernadette spoke, her voice was a lot gentler and more curious than before. "And why do you like to take control?"

He huffed out a laugh. It wasn't a simple question to answer. None of the stereotypes she might think of fit him. He'd never suffered from a loss or lack of control that he was now trying to regain through BDSM. He just found it rewarding to be trusted enough to take care of the women he was with. He couldn't help but recall the look of wonder in Jessica's eyes when he made her come, or the rush of adrenaline when she fell apart beneath him, completely at his mercy.

"I don't know, I just do. It's something I was introduced to in my twenties, and it appealed to me. I've met a lot of amazing people. There are more independent and successful women in BDSM than you might imagine, and many of them are submissives, though there are certainly a lot of dommes, too. It's a community I belong to and that respects me."

Bernadette's expression told him that she'd heard the bitterness that had colored his last sentence. Bitterness left over from his family's quick judgment.

"I'm sorry."

He turned back into the room now, trying to see what Bernadette meant.

"I'm sorry that I didn't believe in you right away. That it took me this long to come see you. And that I let you move away from your family, making you feel like you didn't belong to us anymore."

"What, so all of a sudden you think what I do is all right?"

Bernadette shook her head. "I won't pretend I understand yet, but I'm willing to keep listening. I shouldn't have believed that you were abusing women. It didn't feel right, and I should have listened to that feeling, but I was in shock. I don't know how to feel about any of this yet. I think I'll go to a hotel for the night and maybe tomorrow you're up for meeting with me again and we can keep talking."

Benjamin knew he shouldn't ask. He really knew better, but he couldn't keep the words from coming out. "What about dad?"

Bernadette looked uncomfortable. "Dad doesn't know I'm here."

He nodded. He supposed he should be grateful that at least one member of his family hadn't written him off entirely, but he felt too drained to give it any more thought right now. Instead, he just helped his sister bring her suitcase to her rental car and returned to his empty house.

Maybe he should have offered her to stay in his guest room, but he just didn't feel he had the energy to keep talking all afternoon, and being in this house together without talking would have felt awkward.

His eyes wandered to the dining table that still held the half eaten plates from lunch, his annoyance flaring up again. Maybe his sister would come around, but that wouldn't change that Jessica had left him to defend himself alone. Just like Victoria had done.

Now, he hadn't only lost the chance to be with Jessica, but he'd also need to look for a new club, because he didn't think he could bear seeing her each weekend, knowing he couldn't have her. Couldn't have her, because she wasn't willing to actually commit to him. The pain he felt at that realization stung, because sometime over thc past weeks, sometime last night, he'd thought that he'd finally found someone whom he wanted to share his life with. Someone he could fall in love with so very easily.

And maybe that's why it felt so painful right now. Maybe he'd already fallen in love with her.

CHAPTER FIFTEEN

The first thing Jessica did the next morning was to check her phone.

By the time she'd made it home yesterday, she'd calmed down enough to realize that she'd done the one thing she'd been doing over and over when things got more intense with a dom. She'd retreated and avoided testing the inner voice that told her whom she could trust.

Once she'd been calmer, she'd considered what she knew about Benjamin, and nothing she'd seen him do or hear him say had ever suggested he would force her into anything she didn't want to do. If he'd had a slave in the past, it had no doubt been a consensual relationship, and if he'd still wanted that type of relationship now, he would have told her as much. Nothing but the brunette's comments had ever suggested that he wasn't trustworthy.

She'd send him a text once she'd arrived home, snuggled into the blanket on her bed. In a few words, she'd let him know that she'd arrived safely back at her place and asked him if he was doing okay after the strange confrontation, but all last night she hadn't received a response from him.

She'd stayed up late, hoping he'd write back and they could agree on a time to talk, giving her a chance to explain why she'd stormed out the way she had. Except even this morning, no new messages had appeared on her phone. He still hadn't answered.

He'd told her if she left, they'd be done.

She knew it hadn't been fair for him to say that, but she clung to the hope that he'd just said the words in the heat of the moment and had had a chance to re-think his ultimatum. They were adults, and sometimes things were said that you regretted later.

Adding an extra splash of creamer to her coffee—because mornings like this required added comfort—, Jessica walked down the stairs to her office. It was Monday morning and she should go over the bar's inventory today, placing the orders for the re-supplies needed for the club with the vendors.

She doubted she could focus on a single number, so she sat down behind her desk and stared at her mug for a moment. Then she pulled her phone out again.

For a second, her thumb hovered over the messaging icon, then she scrolled through her phone book instead. When she tapped on his name, she took a deep, calming breath. She'd tell him how his ultimatum had made her feel and ask him if they could meet up to continue their conversation. It was the best she could do right now.

"Hello." His voice was clipped and Jessica suppressed the urge to bite her lip.

"Hello, it's Jessica," she paused, but he didn't speak. "I hope I'm not interrupting your work, but I needed to speak with you. Yesterday didn't go as I'd hoped, and I was wondering if you'd like to get together this week and talk."

A brief pause followed. "I told you how I felt about this already. You heard what my sister said to me, and even after I made it clear that I needed you to stay and support me, you just left. You made your lack of commitment to me clear. I'm no longer interested." The line clicked and Jessica dropped her phone on the table.

That had been cold. He'd just hung up on her.

But why?

Well, that answer was simple enough. She'd done this to herself. Benjamin had told her he wanted a relationship and at the first possible opportunity she'd let her past come between them. She'd listened to what the woman had said and had made assumptions, not even sticking around long enough to learn the brunette was his sister. Assumptions that now that she thought about them didn't sound like Benjamin at all.

Jessica shook her head.

Maybe she'd misread some things, but none of it justified the ultimatum he'd given her. That hadn't been fair to her, and she deserved an apology. Of course, she couldn't blame him for feeling hurt. She'd just walked away when his own sister had accused him of holding her there against her will. She hadn't supported him, instead she'd fled right back into her own hang-ups. It truly was a mess.

And now it was too late to fix it. He didn't even want to talk to her anymore.

The rest of the day went by slowly, and Jessica was fully aware she was sulking. She kept going back and forth between getting mad about Benjamin's ultimatum and rudeness on the phone, and feeling terrible about walking out at a time when he'd needed her support. Again and again she kept coming back to the one thing that bothered her the most. She'd missed out on an opportunity she probably wouldn't find again.

She'd found a dom who'd matched her kinks, had been willing to take things slow and discover how far they both wanted to push their power dynamic. And she'd fallen in love with him.

And then one stupid choice of hers had made him turn his back on them.

Exiting out of the program she'd been using to place her orders, she hoped they'd get the correct bottles delivered on Thursday. She couldn't be entirely sure, since she'd been too distracted all day to give her job the attention it deserved.

There was only one thing she was sure about after this crummy day, and that was that she wouldn't let Benjamin take this away from them because she'd made one wrong choice. He'd have to at least listen to her long enough so she could explain herself to him.

Not wanting to go back up to her apartment to get her purse, she grabbed the back-up car keys from the drawer of her desk.

Just as she was about to get up and drive to Benjamin's place, where he wouldn't be able to just hang up on her, the office phone rang. The number wasn't one she'd saved and the momentary hope that it might be him dissipated. His number would have come up with his name, since she'd saved Benjamin's home and cell number in the office phone, just like she did for every club member.

"This is Jessica at Club B. How can I help you?"

"Uh, yes, hello." The woman's voice sounded hesitant. "This is Bernadette Hoffinger. We kind of met yesterday. I doubt I made a very good impression on you, but I was wondering whether you might be willing to speak with me. Please? I could come out to your area, if you like."

Benjamin's sister wanted to speak to her? All Jessica wanted was to speak to Benjamin himself, so they had a chance to make up, but how could she say no? When the woman had confronted Benjamin yesterday, she'd probably been thinking that she was helping Jessica. Jessica decided to give her the benefit of the doubt and assume her intrusion the previous evening had been misguided but well-intentioned.

Bernadette seemed to misinterpret Jessica's pause as a refusal and started talking again. "I had breakfast with Benjamin today. We spoke and I think I understand a bit better, you know, about what he does, but... I think it would help to hear it from a woman."

Bernadette's voice sounded embarrassed, but also de- termined, and Jessica couldn't help but like the woman's fervent passion to make sure the submissives her brother was with were treated well. If all women looked out for each other that way, a lot of bad situations could prob- ably be prevented. On the other hand, she could also understand the hurt she'd seen in Benjamin's expression yesterday. How would it feel to have your own family treat you like you might be an abuser?

The last thought made Jessica's tone come out steelier than she'd intended. "Are you at Benjamin's place?"

"No, I'm in a hotel, actually."

"I can meet you at the hotel bar in an hour if you let me know where you're staying."

She wrote the name of the hotel down and ended the call. It looked like instead of speaking with Benjamin, she'd first meet with his sister.

When Jessica arrived at the hotel, Bernadette was already sitting at the bar. Their eyes met, and Benjamin's sister rose to greet her.

Now that she knew they were related, Jessica could see some similarities. Not only was Bernadette almost as tall as her brother, but her hair color and eyes matched Benjamin's exactly.

"Thank you for coming. Can I get you a drink?" the woman offered, looking slightly uncomfortable.

"Just a coke, thanks."

Once the bartender had handed Jessica her drink, they headed to the back of the room where several booths stood empty, giving them some privacy.

Instead of letting Bernadette start the conversation off with her own questions, Jessica spoke first. "Yesterday, you said a few things to your brother that were quite damning. You know him for a much longer time than I do, so if you truly believe he abuses women and doesn't respect consent in his BDSM relationships, please explain it to me."

She leveled her gaze at Bernadette, willing her to understand that while she was open to listen to reasonable concerns, she wouldn't tolerate accusations based on prejudice. "I appreciate that you stand up for women's safety, because abuse is terrible and too many women suffer from it, including within the BDSM community, but from what I know about your brother he is a really great guy and wouldn't do something like ignoring a woman's right to leave a relationship. If you have good reason to think I'm wrong, please tell me, but nothing he's ever done with me has been non-consensual."

She'd had some time during the drive to consider Benjamin's words on the phone this morning. He'd said that he'd needed her to stay and support him, and now that she knew who Bernadette was, everything made so much more sense. Jessica was intent on finding out what had happened with his family. If she could help Bernadette understand how much her behavior was hurting Benjamin, it might be enough to prove to him that she was there to support him.

As much as she'd doubted her own ability to judge characters before, she was now sure that she wasn't wrong about Benjamin in this case, and his sister's being here told Jessica that Bernadette was doubting her own accusations as well.

"I knew nothing about him being into this stuff until about two months ago. We were always close, but I guess this isn't really what you talk to your little sister about." She laughed uncomfortably.

"I found out about him being into this stuff when my dad and I accidentally surprised him with his girlfriend. We'd let ourselves into his place and he came home with his girlfriend a little after we'd arrived. It's a long story, but suffice it to say, it was terrible timing."

Before she spoke again, Bernadette's eyes flew around the room as if checking that they were truly out of everyone's earshot. "Anyway, his girlfriend was naked on her knees and he said something about spanking her. I don't remember what he said exactly, but it just sounded so wrong." Bernadette made a disgusted face, and this time, Jessica couldn't blame her. It wasn't like she'd want to find her brother in a compromising position herself.

"I couldn't see her face, just him holding up his hand as if he was ready to hit her."

Jessica tried to imagine the scene, but the thought of Benjamin with another woman kneeling by his feet was enough to make her stop and focus on Bernadette's pleading face instead. It was obvious the other woman

169

was begging her to understand why she'd unjustly accused her own brother of beating women.

As difficult as Jessica found it to believe, it seemed that Bernadette had obviously been shocked and confused by what she'd seen that day. Still, Jessica had to ask. "That can't have been the first time you heard about people doing something kinky in the bedroom, though. Especially not something as simple as a spanking."

The whole thing sounded pretty tame, actually, although Jessica figured she probably wasn't the best judge of things considering her occupation.

"Well, no." Bernadette said. "And I think I wouldn't have let it get so out of hand if it hadn't been for Victoria's resignation the next day."

Jessica raised her eyebrows in question.

"Victoria was Ben's girlfriend, and when she realized we'd seen her she just grabbed her coat and ran out the door. We knew her even before she'd started to date my brother, because she was working for my dad as a customer liaison at the time, which is how she and Ben met, I guess. But then, the morning after it happened, dad got an email from her. She'd written that she was quitting effective immediately and that she couldn't live with the shame. She wrote that she wasn't prepared to continue to be with Benjamin, and that under the circumstances she was actually moving back home to stay with her parents in Colorado."

Bernadette looked at Jessica, her expression earnest. "I mean, it really sounded like she moved across states to get away from Ben. What were we supposed to think?"

"Did you give your brother a chance to explain?"

"He tried to, I guess. After Victoria ran out, Ben told us he was into BDSM and how Victoria had wanted him to hit her. It still sounded pretty messed up, and my dad stormed out of the house, so I went after him. On the drive home, he kept mumbling about how he thought he'd raised a better son. It was pretty bad," Bernadette sighed.

"You've got to know that my dad was a cop until he got a knee injury. After that, he opened a security company. One of the things they do is to take a few cases on for free each year through this non-profit organization that helps women in abusive relationships. When these women leave, oftentimes they don't feel safe, so my dad's company helps them with setting up security, even body guards for things like court appointments and such. It's all because as a cop he got called to a ton of domestic incidents and then... Well, I think the idea of his son hitting a woman just didn't sit well with him and that was all he could think about."

The enormity of the situation hit Jessica. "So your father dumped Benjamin into the same bucket of abusers that he despised, and you believed the same thing?"

Most sexually active people Jessica knew had at least dabbled with BDSM elements, like tying someone up or even some light spanking. It seemed strange that someone could react so shocked to what had probably been a pretty light scene situation, maybe even a funishment. She had to wonder how Benjamin and Bernadette had been raised for this woman to be so clueless about the possibility of adding spice to a relationship.

"When dad and I got home, I realized I shouldn't have just run out after dad without talking to Ben and trying to understand." Bernadette's face was now full of regret and Jessica almost groaned. It looked like she'd done the same thing to Benjamin that his ex and his sister had done, too. They'd all walked out on him when things got uncomfortable. But Bernadette kept speaking, and

Jessica didn't have time to think about the implications of what she'd just learned.

"It wasn't like I suddenly understood why he was into BDSM, or anything, but I decided to call him the next morning. But then dad showed me that email, and I thought Victoria had run from him."

Bernadette looked down at the table, creases forming between her eyes. "So, yeah, I guess I ended up believing the same thing dad did. And then, a month later, Ben moved away, and it was like we'd lost a piece of our family for good."

"More like you broke off a piece, it seems."

"Maybe," Bernadette agreed. "Ben and I spoke about the email this morning and he pointed out that Victoria could've meant that she was ashamed to return to work after her boss stormed out of the house when he saw her in a compromising position with his son. He said, she may have been worried about having to ask for references after being outed as a submissive and decided to move back home where she could get away from the drama."

"And do you believe him?" Jessica asked, keeping her voice gentle.

"I should have." Bernadette looked like she was going to cry. "I guess I can't stop hurting him. Can you believe that I insisted on calling her?"

"So you spoke with Victoria?" Jessica couldn't quite suppress the incredulity in her voice.

"No, I didn't. Her old cell number is inactive, so I couldn't reach her. Instead, I called you."

"Did Benjamin give you my number?" Hope welled up in Jessica. If he'd given Bernadette her number at Club B, didn't that mean he trusted her enough to set things right with his sister?

"No, but he mentioned that you own a BDSM club. It didn't take much to find your website."

Disappointment rushed through her, but Jessica pushed it aside. "Well, I can't tell you what Victoria was thinking, but I can tell you that Benjamin is a very well-respected member in our community. He has a reputation for being ethical, always respecting safe words, and being a generous dom."

Bernadette looked torn for a moment before she asked, "And are you and Ben seeing each other? I mean, is being with him something you like?"

Jessica almost laughed, despite the bitter twinge of regret she felt at the question. "I think I messed up and now he isn't interested in me anymore, but yes, I loved spending time with him. Submission is something that is very fulfilling for me. I enjoy giving up control and being taken care of. It's not something I'm ashamed of or that I would change if I could. Still, I think it's quite possible that Victoria may have felt uncomfortable about her employer knowing what she was into. Many people keep their interest in BDSM hidden for good reason."

They talked for another thirty minutes, and when Jessica walked away, she was hopeful that they'd found a way to prove to Benjamin that despite the mistakes and assumptions they'd made, they were both willing to commit to their love for him, albeit different types of love.

Of course, Bernadette didn't know that the plan was as much about Jessica as it was about her.

CHAPTER SIXTEEN

On Wednesday, Benjamin walked into Club B feeling on edge. Jeffrey had requested he meet him at the club, and despite Benjamin's better judgment, he'd eventually agreed. He knew it was masochistic to come here. Being around Jessica would be like shoving a painful wedge into his heart, and yet he hadn't been able to resist the temptation of seeing her.

After breakfast with his sister on Monday, his anger had slowly cooled. Bernadette had still been doubtful, and that hurt more than he wanted to think about just now, but after he'd gotten that conversation over with, he'd had time to consider Jessica's actions. He'd been so furious that she'd run out when confronted with his family that he'd compared her to Victoria. Except with some of the anger having faded, he'd realized how difficult the situation must have been for her. His sister's accusations would have hit right where Jessica carried her deepest anxieties, courtesy of her ass of an ex fiancé.

And then, when she'd called to talk to him, he'd just cut her off, denying her the one thing he'd been furious about when it had been denied to him. He hadn't given her the chance to explain herself.

When he'd gone to bed on Monday night, alone, he'd realized another thing. On Sunday morning he'd wanted nothing more than to convince Jessica to give him a shot at being her dom, and those feelings of desire and longing toward her hadn't changed. He wanted her in his life, and he knew he'd done the one thing that would ensure that she wouldn't trust him enough to give him a second opportunity.

He'd given her an ultimatum and had thereby done the very thing her ex had done as well. He'd made a demand that had probably made her feel trapped. And that after she'd been brave enough to tell him about how difficult it had been for her to open herself up again. What a great dom he was.

He half expected to have John tell him that his membership had been canceled, but when he stepped into the reception area of Club B, the security guard just waved him through. Inside the club's main room, Benjamin kept his eyes open for Jessica. Because of her height, he might easily miss her in a crowd, but he couldn't help but hope to catch a glimpse of her. Instead, his eyes caught Jeffrey's.

The dom waved him over, and Benjamin made his way to the table near the bar where Jeffrey was sitting with a woman who Benjamin guessed was the sadists' sub for the night.

"Master Benjamin, just the dom I wanted to speak with."

"May I?" Benjamin asked as he pulled one of the empty chairs out.

Jeffrey laughed. "I wouldn't dare say no. You're looking mighty grumpy, my friend."

"You said you wanted to meet in person about the items I want to order?" Not that Benjamin had come here because he was in a rush to order anything for his dungeon. The thought of not being able to test the new furniture out with Jessica being half the reason he was in a grumpy mood. The other half was the thought that she probably wouldn't spend any other time with him, either.

"That is what I said, isn't it?" Jeffrey asked in an annoyingly joking tone. Somehow, the idea that the sadist was having fun on his account raised Benjamin's suspicion.

"I've brought the catalog for you, but I left it outside. Do you want to order a drink first?"

"No, I'm good, thanks." Benjamin still looked over at the bar, to see if perhaps Jessica had shown up. She hadn't.

Jeffrey said something to his sub, and Benjamin turned back to them. The woman got up and walked away with a small smile in Benjamin's direction.

"Since you don't want to get a drink, let's see what else is available for your enjoyment. Come on, I'll show you." The dom got up and, without waiting for a response, started walking toward the door.

Annoyed, Benjamin got up too. He didn't particularly like following other doms around, especially since Jeffrey could have just brought the damn catalog in here. What was he planning? Have Benjamin sit out in his car to look at it?

"What, you didn't want to put the catalog in your toy bag?" he asked as he caught up with Jeffrey.

Jeffrey just grinned, but didn't answer. The sadist opened the door to the entrance area, where John was busy checking in more people, but instead of heading to the front door that led to the parking lot, Jeffrey turned toward Jessica's office and Benjamin's suspicion increased.

When Jeffrey opened the door and stepped back instead of walking through, a sliver of hope rose in Benjamin. He'd see Jessica. Perhaps she'd cancel his membership, but somehow he didn't think she would. All she ever did was make people feel safe in her club. Be inclusive. But then again, the way he'd acted and the things he'd said to her had been unacceptable. Maybe more than she was willing to tolerate from someone in her club.

He stepped in and froze. Instead of Jessica, the first person he saw was his sister.

"Hey Ben." Bernadette rose from her place on the love seat. "Can we talk?"

He'd thought his sister had left town after their breakfast on Monday. Had assumed that she'd come to hear him out and then left to stew over his explanations. It wasn't as if she'd fallen into his arms to apologize and tell him she'd misjudged him after he'd finally had the chance to explain himself. So what was she doing in Jessica's office, of all places?

After hearing about the stupid email Victoria had sent, he could at least understand some of the confusion Bernadette must have felt. His ex had used some really poor phrasing. He didn't think she'd done it intentionally, probably not even thinking that his family would jump to such crazy assumptions about him. After all, what his sister and father had seen had been a fun interaction between them, not something involving any violence. At least not as they'd experienced it. Victoria had probably been embarrassed and maybe ashamed, and Benjamin wouldn't hold it against her.

"What are you doing here?" Seeing his sister in a BDSM club had never been high on his bucket list. At least, she wasn't in the actual club where they'd be surrounded by people in fet wear, or worse, naked and doing scenes. That would have meant he'd have to bleach his brain and his eyes afterward, something he would happily avoid.

"I'm here to apologize."

"You are?" He couldn't help the disbelief in his voice. Despite having grown up together, nothing he'd said on Monday had actually convinced Bernadette that her prejudices had been unfounded, and now she was sitting in Club B, ready to apologize.

"Yes, I am."

Twenty minutes later, he'd heard about Bernadette's meeting with Jessica and how Jessica had invited Bernadette to speak to some female submissives from Club B today. Not only had his sister's apology been sincere, but she'd also told him that she'd speak to their dad on his behalf. While Benjamin didn't need his sister to fight his battles, it had helped him realize one thing. While his father and sister had acted poorly, he'd acted like a petulant teenager too, refusing to stand up for himself. Instead, he'd moved to Canada.

He didn't regret the move. It hadn't been an entirely spur-of-the-moment decision after all, but the timing had been based on his feeling resentful toward his family. Since he had done nothing wrong, he shouldn't have run away as if he'd been trying to hide something. Something else that had added to his sister's doubt in him.

Eventually his sister said her goodbye, which included the explanation that while she understood better now why he did what he did as a dom, she absolutely, under no circumstances, wanted to witness anything behind the club's doors if he was present. He couldn't blame her. So, he walked her to her rental and promised to take her to breakfast again the next morning before she'd catch a flight back home.

As he walked back into Club B this time, he no longer felt on edge, instead, he felt determined. He'd screwed up with Jessica, but she'd still met his sister and helped him by not only explaining things to Bernadette from a submissive's perspective, she'd done even more and set up this entire meeting to make sure he could have his family back. It was more than he'd ever hoped for, and he felt a wave of possessiveness toward this woman who stood up for herself and others in a way that was brave, impressive, and absolutely beautiful.

He also knew that if she'd wanted to see him, she would have known where to find him. The fact that she hadn't come told him he had some serious making up to do.

"Hey John, can you tell me where Jessica is right now?" He tried to glance at the surveillance cameras, but they were shielded from this side of the reception desk.

"I could," John said, "but can you tell me that you won't make her regret seeing you?"

He was sure John could see the surprise on his face. The security guard had never been anything but friendly and easygoing with him, even earlier today. His question now came out of left field.

"I can promise I'll do right by her," he said, giving the man across from him a stern stare. "The rest is up to Jessica. She's a damn strong woman, so you bet she wouldn't let me get away with anything less."

"I am strong," Jessica said from her office, "but I'd rather *you* didn't let *me* get away with anything."

He turned to look at her. She was standing in her office door, wearing a skimpy red skirt and a matching lace bralette. Her brown curls were framing her face, and she looked stunning.

"Can we talk?"

She tilted her head slightly, as if considering his request. "Come with me."

Closing her office door, she headed across the entrance area to the club. Once inside, she kept walking through the crowd until she got to the private rooms.

She opened a door and stepped through, not bothering to check whether it was occupied.

Benjamin had never played in this particular room, though he'd seen it during his monitoring shifts. The walls were the same as the main club room, giving the impression of cave walls. The rest of the space was fairly empty, except for a large sex swing that hung in the middle of the room. There were no other chairs or seating opportunities in the room, and he wondered what the little submissive had in mind coming here.

That the choice of room was intentional had been clear the second he'd spotted the reserved sign on the door as he'd followed her inside.

When she turned around, Jessica looked determined to give him a piece of her mind, and despite everything that had gone wrong, he had to suppress a grin. Considering she'd been worried about misreading men and getting herself caught up in a situation she wasn't prepared for, this woman was probably the most confident and strong submissive he'd ever met. He knew that she wouldn't tolerate anything that didn't feel right to her, and the fact that she'd had to prove that once already in the past was enough to make him want to protect her with everything he had.

She'd planned on speaking with him here, not in her office, and that made him more hopeful than he had a right to be after the way he'd hung up on her on Monday.

"You were wrong to give me an ultimatum. It wasn't fair to do that, and I hope you regret it." The words were cutting, but he didn't think she'd intended that last part to be hurtful. She was truly just hoping that he'd thought about his actions and had realized he'd been wrong to say those words to her. He kept his expression neutral, simply nodding. Because she was right, he did regret them.

Apparently, it wasn't the reaction she'd expected, because her eyes grew bigger and she didn't continue berating him. She just stood there looking at him, and he wanted nothing more than to receive her forgiveness and make her trust him again.

"You're right, little one. I shouldn't have said that, and I regret those words. Please accept my apology. I understand that I'll need to keep earning your trust back after what happened, but if you'll give me a chance I am prepared to do just that."

"You are?" The hopefulness in her expression was all the invitation he needed. He stalked toward her, stopping right in front of her to lean down slightly, bringing his mouth to her ear.

"We have much to discuss, little one, but right now, unless you tell me your safe word, I will kiss you."

She said nothing, just waited for him to act.

He moved slowly at first, trailing kisses down her jawline until he reached her mouth, then all his restraint broke and he kissed her so fiercely, they might both walk away with bruised lips.

Eventually, she pulled back, and he released her. They were both panting, and her skin was slightly flushed.

"I didn't know Bernadette was your sister, and I didn't want to believe the things she'd said, but I needed some space to think and evaluate my own reaction. When I arrived at home, I'd already realized that it didn't sound right, that I didn't think you'd ever do that, but I told you I'm working through these trust issues and I can't promise they'll disappear overnight."

"No, they won't, so I'll start fighting them today," he promised. "I'll fight those fears with you, because I want you, little one. And if you agree, I'll make you mine and protect you for as long as you'll have me."

He wrapped his hands around her back and pulled her closer until her belly was pressed against his erection. This was about more than sex, but after he'd almost ruined this once already, he wasn't prepared to take any chances this time. He needed Jessica to understand how much he desired her. How much he already loved her, because that was what this was.

He'd never met a more impressive woman in his life, and he wanted to get to know her better every single day. Wanted to make her his to explore and keep.

Benjamin's eyes were hooded with passion, but the sincerity in them shone through clearly. Jessica stared into them as she let herself sink more against him, pressing her breasts against his warm body.

He was offering her everything she'd ever wanted. A dom who wanted to cherish her and gift himself to her to care for, in turn. Real life didn't disappear, but with Benjamin, it felt like she could conquer anything. He wanted to have her, and nothing in the world could have stopped her from agreeing, because she didn't doubt that he would keep her safe.

They might have to work through things, get to know each other better and negotiate their relationship and D/s dynamic, but she wanted the chance to do that. To figure out what life with Benjamin would look like.

She said the only thing that made sense. "I want you, Benjamin. Please, make me yours, sir."

His answering groan was in perfect harmony with her moan as his lips landed on hers again. She melted against him, not caring about anything but the feel of his lips on hers, his arms around her, and the evidence of his arousal pressed against her belly. This was the moment she'd longed for since she'd realized what she may have lost on Sunday.

When he took her shoulders and pushed her back slightly, she smiled at him lazily. She knew he'd take charge now, and the relief was almost as heady as the other feelings rushing through her. Trust, anticipation, love.

"You chose this room, little one, so I think we better put it to good use." Grabbing her by the waist, Benjamin pushed her backward until she could feel the sex swing in her back.

"Jump up, darling." He lifted her up until her butt settled into the swing. It was a purchase she'd made last year. The swing had a full seat, with restraints for hands and legs, which Benjamin immediately got to work buckling around her wrists and ankles. All the while, he trailed kisses over her body. She was still wearing her bralette and skirt, and right now she would have happily ripped the fabric off her body, though Benjamin didn't seem concerned by it.

When he stepped in front of her, his look was intense, and shivers ran across her skin in waves.

"You're mine, little one, and I'll remind you of that now. When we walk out of this room, everyone will see that I've claimed you." His eyes caught hers. "You've told me before that you didn't want permanent marks. Are you okay with temporary ones?"

183

"I'm green, sir," she answered, need rushing through her. He wanted to claim her, and the thought of seeing his marks on her was making her grow wet and desperate for his touch.

He reached out for the swing's electric control panel that hung from the ceiling, and with a humming noise the swing started to rise higher into the air, until Jessica found herself at the height of Benjamin's shoulders. When he leaned forward and flipped her skirt up, she held her breath until his mouth found the sensitive skin on the inside of her thigh, placing gentle kisses on her that send electrical sparks up to her pussy.

Her feet were in stirrups, and her ankles secured to the suspension ropes of the swing, leaving her legs spread and her pussy available. Even through the thin fabric of her thong, she could feel the rush of his hot breath against her. Then, he lowered his mouth again, sucking at her inner thigh, while his hands started to stroke her legs. He stayed like that for a while, the slight pulling of his sucking motion on her skin driving her mad. When he lifted his head, a small red mark showed on her skin. At the sight, her core tensed and arousal washed over her.

She needed his touch, and she wasn't above begging. She pleaded with him and moaned for him, wanting nothing more than for his mouth to land on her clit, sucking there as he'd sucked on her thigh, but Benjamin ignored her pleading. Instead, he spun the swing around until she was sideways.

He pulled her bralette up over her head until it was wrapped around her head and arms, covering her eyes like a blindfold would. Then, his mouth landed on her right nipple, sucking, and the sensation sent her over, an unexpected orgasm making her cry out his name.

"Beautiful, little one. I love hearing you moan my name."

She lay there, panting, as he simply continued to lather her with kisses, occasionally stopping to leave little red marks on her breasts, stomach, shoulders, and neck. It was maddening and arousing, and it would've been perfect if he'd only touch her where she needed it the most, but Benjamin took his time, and she knew she was his to explore.

She leaned her head back and allowed him to do what he wished, driving her to insanity as he touched and teased every inch of her exposed skin until he moved her thong to the side and his mouth finally landed on her most private place. She came apart beneath him and knew that when she became whole again, he would always be a part of her.

When she finally caught her breath, her senses returning to her body, she heard the noise of the swing lowering.

"Are you ready for me, little one?"

"Oh god, yes. Please, Benjamin. Please, sir."

He pressed into her, using the swing to rock her onto his thick erection. She wanted to touch him, but her wrists were still cuffed above her head.

"Please, please, I want to touch you."

"No." He pulled her further against him, sheathing himself completely inside her.

"Then please let me see you," she pleaded. Her bralette was still pulled over her eyes, blindfolding her, and she desperately needed another connection to him.

"Maybe," he said, his voice teasing, then he pushed her back off his cock and yanked her against him, making her muscles quiver. He felt so good inside her, and her recent

185

orgasms had left her swollen and sensitive to the friction he was creating.

"Tell me who you want to belong to." He started moving her back and forth, using a fierce rhythm.

"You, sir. Oh, Benjamin, I want to belong to you."

He pulled the bralette from her eyes and she could finally see him. At the same moment, he reached for something that had hung from a hook on the swing. A moment later she heard a humming noise, then he pressed a vibrator directly on her clit. She came again, staring into his face. Only seconds later, Benjamin yanked her hard against him and he came as well, calling her name as he shuttered his release.

Epilogue

F our weeks later, Jessica followed Benjamin off a plane in Los Angeles. Bernadette had invited them to her place for a family barbecue, and it was the first time Benjamin was going to see his father again.

Benjamin's and her relationship was going incredibly well and besides the phenomenal sex, Jessica felt much less stressed, not only about trying to find a dom, which was no longer an issue since Benjamin filled that role amazingly, but also about her daily routine at the club. She'd always enjoyed running the club, but things had overwhelmed her lately. Since he checked in with her throughout the day, Benjamin had picked up on things that had been weighing her down, like the pressure of prioritizing her tasks correctly to get everything done.

Much to her surprise, he'd insisted on scheduling a call each morning where she told him the items she needed to do during the day and they set a task list, which she worked off over the course of the day, sending him a message each time she'd accomplished something. Now, she never felt like she was just wading through mud anymore. Instead, she could celebrate each little thing she checked off her list, and whenever she'd been especially productive, Benjamin came up with ways to reward her.

They'd only been together for a short time, but she couldn't be happier, so when he'd asked whether she'd accompany him to L.A., she'd recruited her best friend to baby-sit her club for the weekend and had agreed. Of course, she was nervous about meeting Benjamin's father, but she'd never hidden when someone had critiqued her lifestyle before and she wasn't about to do that now. Especially not when her dom needed her.

It took them forty-five minutes to get to their accommodations, but when they finally arrived, Jessica realized that Benjamin had splurged on a small suite in the luxurious hotel. When he opened the door with the key card they'd received at the reception desk, Jessica spotted a chilled bottle of champagne waiting for them and her heart beat faster. She'd never needed a man to shower her with lavish gifts—she made enough money to buy herself the things she wanted—, but it was knowing that Benjamin had done this to make her happy that caused her smile to widen.

Even though they'd spent quite a few nights together since she'd agreed to be his, spending a weekend in a hotel felt different and Jessica had brought some new lingerie that she was excited to show Benjamin. Either they would celebrate a successful trip, or she'd help get his mind off of things if something went south during tomorrow's barbecue.

The door fell shut behind them and Benjamin gave her a predatory smile. "Strip, little one."

He didn't have to tell her twice. She quickly took off her clothes, folding them neatly into a pile, and stood in front of him in the way he'd told her he liked. Feet shoulder width apart, hands behind her back.

"Come with me." He held his hand out and she took it, allowing him to pull her toward the table with the champagne bottle. Opening it, he poured them each a glass. "To my beautiful little submissive."

Happiness bubbled in her, as if trying to keep up with the sparkling drink in her glass. "To my wonderful dom," she answered, and his smile made the skin around his eyes crinkle in that way she loved so much.

"Wait here while I bring our suitcases into the bedroom." He disappeared and Jessica sipped her champagne, content to just listen to his movements in the other room. She could hear the zipper of a suitcase being opened, then his footsteps returning to her.

When he walked in, he'd taken off his sweater, wearing a light blue dress shirt and jeans. He was mouthwateringly handsome, and Jessica was more than happy to be naked already. She wanted to feel his hands on her and strip him of his own clothes, allowing her access to his hot body.

He met her hungry gaze and pulled her against him, placing a demanding kiss against her lips, before pushing her back.

"I've made dinner reservations for us in two hours. Until then, we have much to do."

"What is that, sir?"

His answering grin sent the bubbles floating inside her stomach downward, pooling low in her core.

"Well, first, I want you to lean over the back of that couch over there."

Jessica followed his direction, settling her upper body over the backrest of the couch, leaving her exposed bottom pushed backward for him. She arched her back, and his hands started to fondle her, quickly driving her wild with the way his fingers dipped in and out of her. He stroked her folds and teased her clit as if he had no intention of doing anything but this for the next couple of hours until they needed to go to dinner.

When she tried to move backward and push herself further against his hand, he swatted her butt cheek. The sting of his hand raced to her clit, making her ache even more.

She was more than ready for him, but he was still wearing his jeans. "Please, sir, please take me."

"I don't think so, little one. I dislike it when I'm being rushed."

He went down on his knees, torturing her all over again, this time using his mouth until an orgasm shattered her restraint and she begged him for his cock once more.

"So needy," he teased. "Now tell me, little one. What do you want more? Do you want me to fuck you right now, take you hard until you come around my cock, or do you want to see the surprise I brought you and then make love afterward?"

Her mind was still spinning from the orgasm and her pussy was clenching rhythmically, desperately waiting to be filled, but his words made her pause. She wanted him badly, but he'd brought a surprise for her and she didn't want to ruin that for him. She also wanted him to fuck her right now, but the way he'd said he would make love to her made her heart ache in need, more powerful than the throbbing of her pussy.

"The surprise and making love, sir, please."

Approval shone through his eyes. "Very good, sweetheart. Come." Once again he held his hand out to her, and she pushed herself off the couch. Her legs a bit wobbly, she allowed him to pull her to the windows of the suite.

Outside was a beautiful view of Manhattan Beach, the water sparkling in the afternoon sun. It was stunning, but Jessica's eyes quickly settled back on her dom.

"Kneel for me." His voice was soft and her legs gave way before she had even a second to think. She landed on the rough carpet and winced slightly.

Benjamin walked over to the couch and picked up one of the decorative pillows, bringing it back and helping her place it under her knees. Then he pulled a rectangular jewelry box out of his back pocket and Jessica's breathing stopped.

"Breathe, little one." He chuckled and went down on one knee in front of her. "We've only been seeing each other for a short time, but I've made you mine and I want you to have a reminder that I'm yours as well. A reminder that I'm there to protect and cherish you, and that I'm there to guide and command you."

He opened the jewelry box so she could see the delicate silver necklace with a small lock charm. It was beautiful and tears pricked her eyes.

"You will wear this as a reminder that you belong to me. Perhaps, sometime in the future, we'll discuss a permanent collar, but for now, I think this day collar will be enough to mark you as mine."

Reaching up, he pushed a lock of her hair back. "What do you say, little one?"

A tear slipped down her cheek as she looked into her dom's eyes.

"Oh, yes, sir. Thank you, it's so beautiful." She couldn't take her eyes off of the tiny silver lock that lay on the black velvet in the box. It represented all her hopes, dreams, and needs, and she couldn't have imagined a more perfect moment. "I'll always wear it."

"Yes, you will. Now tell me who you belong to."

"I'm yours, sir. I belong to you, Benjamin."

He leaned forward to kiss her, and when he moved back minutes later, he'd fastened the collar around her neck.

She was his, and he finally took her, pressed against the window overlooking the water, until they both got lost in each other.

Afterword

Dear Reader,

Thank you for reading *Caught Up In Love*!

If you enjoyed this book, you can keep reading about Club B in *Roped Up In Love*, the third book in this series of standalone romances.

If you have the time, I would sincerely appreciate it if you would leave a review online. Your reviews mean a lot and are incredibly helpful for authors.

Until next time,
C.A. Krause

Printed in Great Britain
by Amazon